The Big Field Trip

Diversity, Equality, and Inclusion

Arden Willowfield

Published by Whimsy Tales Press, 2024.

This is a work of fiction. Similarities to real people, places, or events are entirely coincidental.

THE BIG FIELD TRIP

First edition. November 19, 2024.

Copyright © 2024 Arden Willowfield.

ISBN: 979-8230648116

Written by Arden Willowfield.

Table of Contents

Dedication 1
Preface 2
Chapter 1: The Exciting Announcement 3
Chapter 2: Preparing for the Trip 7
Chapter 3: The Bus Ride to Adventure 12
Chapter 4: First Impressions 16
Chapter 5: Exploring the Art Pavilion 20
Chapter 6: Music Workshop – Rhythms and Beats 24
Chapter 7: Stories from the Heart 28
Chapter 8: Dance of Joy 32
Chapter 9: Trying on Traditional Clothing 37
Chapter 10: Learning New Languages 41
Chapter 11: Tasting Flavors from Around the World 44
Chapter 12: Traditions of Togetherness 48
Chapter 13: Lessons in Craftsmanship 53
Chapter 14: The World of Folktales and Legends 58
Chapter 15: Symbols of Identity and Belonging 63
Chapter 16: Music of the World 68
Chapter 17: The Power of Words and Poetry 72
Chapter 18: Art of the Everyday 76
Chapter 19: Games, Sports, and Team Spirit 80
Chapter 20: Culinary Traditions and Cooking Together .. 84
Chapter 21: Festivals of Light and Color 88
Chapter 22: Dance and Movement as Celebration 92
Chapter 23: Storytelling Circles and Shared Wisdom 96
Chapter 24: Language, Laughter, and Connection 100
Chapter 25: The Closing Circle of Gratitude 105

Dedication

This book is dedicated to young adventurers everywhere, to those who see the world with wonder, compassion, and a curiosity for all that is different and new. May you find beauty in diversity, kindness in every encounter, and the joy of discovering friendships that cross all boundaries. To parents, teachers, and caregivers who nurture these values, thank you for guiding children to be open-hearted explorers. And to the dreamers, the storytellers, the artists, and the creators—thank you for inspiring us all to celebrate our unique colors, rhythms, and voices in the tapestry of life.

Preface

In a world as vast and colorful as ours, children are natural explorers, eager to learn, share, and grow. *The Big Field Trip* was born from a desire to capture this natural curiosity and to share with children a story about diversity, inclusion, and the beauty of human connection. Throughout this story, young readers join a class of students on an incredible field trip to a multicultural festival. Through food, music, dance, and stories, they experience the rich variety of cultures, discovering that while traditions may differ, the values of kindness, friendship, and respect are universal. This book is more than just a story; it's an invitation for young minds to celebrate diversity and to recognize that our differences make the world more vibrant. We hope this book encourages children to seek understanding, spread joy, and build connections with everyone they meet.

Chapter 1: The Exciting Announcement

The day began like any other at Riverside Elementary School. The class was buzzing with chatter, laughter, and the sound of pencils scratching on paper. Ms. Lopez, the beloved fifth-grade teacher, entered the room, her warm smile as bright as the morning sun filtering through the classroom windows. She took a moment to look around the room, watching her students' eager faces as they dove into their morning work. Ms. Lopez had always loved this time of day, but today, she held a secret that made her heart race with anticipation.

When the bell rang, signaling the official start of the school day, Ms. Lopez cleared her throat and called the class to attention. The students glanced up from their work, sensing something special in the air. Ms. Lopez stood at the front of the room with her hands clasped together, her eyes sparkling.

"Good morning, everyone! I have a very exciting announcement to make," she said, her voice laced with excitement.

The room went silent as every student leaned forward, hanging on her every word.

"Next Friday," she continued, "we'll be going on a field trip. But this won't be just any field trip. We've been invited to attend a multicultural festival!"

A wave of excitement rippled through the room. The students exchanged glances, and a few started whispering in excitement. Ms. Lopez paused, letting the news sink in, before raising her hand to quiet the room again.

"This is a very special event," she continued. "The multicultural festival is a celebration where people from many different backgrounds come together to share their traditions, stories, and talents. We'll get to explore art, music, food, clothing, and even languages from all around the world!"

"Wow!" gasped Mia, a girl with bright, curious eyes. "We're going to learn about so many different cultures?"

"Exactly, Mia!" Ms. Lopez replied. "This festival will be a chance for us to appreciate the beauty of diversity. We'll learn not only about the unique traditions of others but also discover how much we have in common, no matter where we come from."

Liam, a thoughtful boy with glasses, raised his hand. "Will we get to try different foods?"

Ms. Lopez chuckled, nodding. "Yes, Liam, you'll have a chance to try foods from various parts of the world. And you'll even get to create some traditional art, learn a few dance moves, and hear stories that have been told for generations."

The excitement in the room grew. Each child's mind filled with visions of the upcoming adventure, wondering what they'd see, hear, taste, and experience. Some were already imagining the sounds of drums, the scent of spices, and the vibrant colors of traditional costumes. Ms. Lopez could see that this announcement had stirred something special in her students. It wasn't just curiosity; it was a spark of open-mindedness, a desire to understand the world beyond their familiar surroundings.

"But," Ms. Lopez continued, raising her hand once more to regain the room's focus, "there's something very important I want to talk to you about before we go."

The students quieted, their gazes fixed on her.

"When we visit the festival, we'll be guests in a space filled with people who may have different ways of doing things, different beliefs, and different ways of celebrating. It's a place where we must be especially respectful. Respect is the most important part of learning about other cultures."

The students nodded, understanding the seriousness in her tone. Many of them had heard the word "respect" before, but Ms. Lopez wanted to make sure they understood it in this context.

"Respect means more than just saying 'please' and 'thank you,'" she explained. "It means keeping an open mind, asking questions in a kind way, and never judging something just because it's different from what you know. It's okay to be curious, and it's okay if you don't understand something right away. But what's important is that we approach everything we see with a spirit of kindness and acceptance."

A hand shot up in the back of the room. It was Ethan, a boy with a mischievous smile who loved asking questions. "Does that mean we shouldn't laugh if something seems strange?"

"That's exactly right, Ethan," Ms. Lopez said, smiling back at him. "Sometimes, things that are new to us might feel strange or even funny because they're unfamiliar. But just because something is new to us doesn't make it silly or wrong. In fact, it's these differences that make our world so beautiful and interesting. Imagine how boring it would be if everyone looked, spoke, and celebrated in the exact same way."

The students murmured in agreement, nodding as they pondered her words.

Ms. Lopez continued, "This trip will be a chance to make connections, to celebrate the differences that make each of us unique, and to find the ways that we're all similar, too. We'll learn that even though people may have different ways of expressing themselves, we all share common values like love, kindness, and friendship."

Just then, Mia raised her hand again, her expression thoughtful. "Ms. Lopez, what if we don't know how to say something the right way or if we accidentally offend someone?"

Ms. Lopez smiled reassuringly. "That's a great question, Mia. We might make mistakes because learning about different cultures can be challenging. But if we approach everything with kindness and humility, people will understand that we're trying our best. Just remember to ask questions if you're unsure and be honest if you don't understand something. People are usually very happy to share their traditions if they see that you're interested and respectful."

At this, a gentle confidence filled the room. The students felt prepared to step outside of their comfort zones, ready to learn and grow. They spent the rest of the morning talking about what they were most excited to see, hear, and taste. Ms. Lopez knew this trip was going to be more than just an educational experience; it would be a life lesson, one that might shape the way her students saw the world forever.

Finally, Ms. Lopez gathered the class into a circle to discuss one last thing. "Since we're going to be experiencing so many new things, I want each of you to keep a small notebook to write down what you learn. After the festival, we'll share our experiences with each other so everyone can hear about what you discovered and what surprised you the most."

As the students gathered in a circle, they felt an invisible bond pulling them closer together. They were a team, a class on a journey of exploration and discovery. Each child felt a little braver, knowing that they had friends by their side who would support them along the way. The excitement in the room was almost tangible, like a vibrant energy bouncing off the walls.

As Ms. Lopez dismissed the class for recess, she heard snippets of conversation drifting out the door. The students were already talking about what they'd wear, what they hoped to see, and what they wanted to learn. Some even speculated about what kinds of foods they might try. It was clear that this trip would not only bring them closer to the world but also to each other.

Chapter 2: Preparing for the Trip

As the day of the multicultural festival approached, the excitement among Ms. Lopez's class continued to build. Each morning, students arrived at school with fresh questions, new ideas, and even a few jitters. For many of them, this would be their first experience with cultures vastly different from their own. Ms. Lopez could feel the enthusiasm radiating from each student, and she knew they were ready for a once-in-a-lifetime adventure. But before they could set off, she wanted to ensure they were as prepared as possible—not just with packed lunches and sturdy shoes, but with open hearts and respectful minds.

The day before the trip, Ms. Lopez decided to dedicate the entire morning to helping her students understand what they would encounter and how they could make the most of the experience. She started the lesson by writing three big words on the board: **Respect, Curiosity, and Open-mindedness.** Turning to the class, she tapped the board lightly, drawing everyone's attention.

"Class," she began, "these three words will be our guiding lights tomorrow. Each one of them will help us experience the festival in a way that's meaningful, respectful, and fun."

The students exchanged intrigued glances. They'd heard these words before, but Ms. Lopez seemed to be giving them special importance now. Their teacher continued, "Today, we're going to talk about how to approach the festival and how to make sure we're the best guests we can be. A big part of that is understanding these three words. So, let's start with 'respect.' Who can tell me what respect means to you?"

Eager hands shot up, and Ms. Lopez called on Jackson, a bright boy who loved to answer questions. "Respect means treating people nicely and not being rude," Jackson said confidently.

"Good start, Jackson!" Ms. Lopez replied. "Respect does mean treating others kindly. But it also means honoring people's traditions, especially when they're different from our own."

Ms. Lopez explained that they might see people doing things differently than they were used to, like dancing in ways they hadn't seen before, speaking in languages they didn't understand, or wearing clothing they had never seen. She wanted them to know that respect was about keeping an open mind and appreciating these differences without making judgments or assumptions.

"We're going to a place where we're visitors, like guests in someone's home," she said. "When we're guests, it's our job to be respectful and to act with kindness. It's okay to be curious, but it's also important to remember that everything we'll see is meaningful to someone. Just as you wouldn't want someone laughing at something that's special to you, we need to be sure we're showing that same respect."

The students nodded thoughtfully. Respect wasn't a new concept, but they were beginning to see it in a new light.

Next, Ms. Lopez tapped the word "Curiosity" on the board. "Who can tell me what curiosity means?" she asked.

This time, Sophia raised her hand. "Curiosity is wanting to know more about something," she said, her eyes shining.

"Exactly," Ms. Lopez said. "Curiosity is about exploring, learning, and asking questions. But here's the thing: there are ways to be curious that are kind, and ways to be curious that can hurt people's feelings. For example, if you see something that looks strange to you, you can ask about it respectfully, like, 'Could you tell me more about this?' rather than saying, 'Why do you do that?' See the difference?"

The students nodded again, some of them mouthing the words Ms. Lopez had used, practicing the gentle tone. She encouraged them to think of curiosity as a door that could be opened carefully, leading to new friendships and understanding. When they showed respectful curiosity, people would feel valued and would often be more than happy to share their stories.

Finally, Ms. Lopez pointed to the last word: "Open-mindedness." She looked around the room, smiling, as if she knew this one might be trickier.

"What does it mean to be open-minded?" she asked, hoping to spark some ideas.

A few students furrowed their brows, and Liam finally spoke up. "Is it like... being okay with things being different?"

"Yes!" Ms. Lopez said, her face lighting up. "Being open-minded means being willing to accept and try to understand things that might be different from what you're used to. It means letting go of the idea that your way is the only way, and being willing to see the world from another person's perspective."

Ms. Lopez explained that open-mindedness would allow them to truly enjoy the festival, seeing everything as a new learning experience instead of something strange or unusual. It was the key to appreciating the festival fully, because with an open mind, they would be able to see the beauty in everything, even if it was unfamiliar.

To help reinforce these ideas, Ms. Lopez decided to do a little role-playing with the class. She invited a few students to the front and handed them scenarios they might encounter at the festival. One scenario involved trying a new food they'd never seen before, another involved hearing a song in a language they didn't understand, and the last involved watching a traditional dance.

Each student acted out how they thought they would respond, and the rest of the class discussed if their reactions showed respect, curiosity, and open-mindedness. It was a fun exercise, and Ms. Lopez could see her students were taking these lessons to heart.

When the role-play ended, Ms. Lopez gathered the class in a circle to discuss some practical things they could do to show respect, curiosity, and open-mindedness. She encouraged them to listen more than they spoke, to ask questions in a kind way, and to be brave enough to try new things, even if they felt nervous. The students came up with a few phrases they could use to show curiosity, like "I'd love to know more about that," or "That sounds interesting; can you tell me more?" Ms. Lopez was thrilled to see how invested they were in learning these skills, knowing it would make their experience at the festival that much richer.

As they discussed, Ms. Lopez noticed a few students still seemed unsure. She asked if anyone had any questions or worries about the festival. Hesitantly, Emma raised her hand.

"What if... what if I don't like the food or the music? Is it rude if I don't want to try everything?" Emma asked, her cheeks turning a little pink.

Ms. Lopez smiled kindly. "That's a great question, Emma. Being open-minded doesn't mean you have to like everything, and it doesn't mean you have to try everything if you're uncomfortable. But it does mean you're willing to give things a chance. If you try a new food and don't like it, that's okay! Just remember to be polite about it. And if you hear music that's different, you don't have to dance if you don't want to. Just listening and showing respect is already wonderful."

Emma nodded, looking relieved. Ms. Lopez reassured her, and the rest of the class, that being respectful was more important than forcing themselves to do something they were uncomfortable with. She explained that their willingness to listen, observe, and appreciate others' traditions was already a sign of respect.

As the morning lesson drew to a close, Ms. Lopez decided to end with a story that showed the beauty of open-mindedness and respect. She told a tale of a young girl who traveled to a faraway village where everything seemed strange and different to her. At first, the girl felt nervous and out of place. But as she spent time with the villagers, she saw that even though they dressed, ate, and spoke differently, they were kind and welcoming. The more she opened her mind, the more she saw that the villagers valued family, kindness, and friendship, just like she did. By the end of her visit, the girl felt as though she had made lifelong friends and had gained a whole new perspective on the world.

Chapter 3: The Bus Ride to Adventure

The morning of the field trip dawned with a crispness in the air that seemed to heighten the excitement bubbling within Ms. Lopez's class. As the students gathered outside Riverside Elementary, they clutched their lunches, chattered excitedly with one another, and tried to catch glimpses of the big yellow bus waiting to take them to the multicultural festival. The anticipation had been building all week, and now that the day had arrived, it felt almost magical. Each student wore a name tag, carefully prepared by Ms. Lopez, with room for them to write something they learned or a new word they discovered during the festival.

When Ms. Lopez arrived to meet them, she carried a bag full of notebooks and pens for each student, a journal where they could record their thoughts, discoveries, and experiences. "Good morning, class!" she greeted them with her warm smile. "Is everyone ready for the adventure?"

A resounding chorus of "Yes!" and "I can't wait!" rang out. Ms. Lopez distributed the notebooks, encouraging each child to jot down things that inspired them, things they found unusual, and anything that made them feel connected to the festival. "This will be like a treasure chest of memories," she explained. "A place to hold all the special things you experience today. By the end of the day, you'll see just how much you've learned and discovered."

As they climbed aboard the bus, Ms. Lopez reminded the students about the values they'd discussed the day before—Respect, Curiosity, and Open-mindedness. "Keep those words in your minds and hearts today," she said. "They'll guide us through this experience and help us see the beauty in everything we encounter."

The bus was alive with energy as it began the journey. Kids settled into their seats, many of them already flipping through their notebooks, ready to fill them with discoveries. A few students craned their necks to look out the windows, hoping to catch a glimpse of where they were headed. Others huddled together, talking excitedly about what they were most looking forward to.

Sitting near the front, Mia turned to her friend Emma. "I can't believe we're actually going! I wonder what the music will be like, or the food. I've never been to a festival like this before."

Emma nodded, her eyes wide with anticipation. "I'm a little nervous," she admitted. "What if I don't understand what people are saying? Or what if something feels too different?"

"That's okay," Mia replied, repeating words they'd heard from Ms. Lopez. "We're here to learn and just enjoy it all. Plus, Ms. Lopez said it's okay if we don't like everything, as long as we're respectful."

A few rows back, Jackson and Ethan were engaged in a different kind of conversation. "Do you think we'll get to try a lot of food?" Jackson asked, his voice full of hope.

Ethan grinned. "I hope so! I'm ready to try anything, even if it's weird. I bet there's something really spicy, like that chili sauce my dad uses."

Nearby, Sophia overheard their conversation and chimed in, "I'm excited for the dancing! I hope we get to learn some cool moves. I've always wanted to try a traditional dance."

As the bus wound its way through town, Ms. Lopez could hear snippets of all these conversations. She was thrilled that each student was so eager to engage in a unique way. She knew that these early conversations were setting the stage for a day of exploration, as each child carried their own hopes, curiosities, and questions. She encouraged them to keep talking, suggesting that they try guessing what the festival might look like and what they might experience when they arrived.

"Let's play a little game," she said, standing up at the front of the bus. "It's called, 'What do you think you'll see?' Imagine we've just stepped off the bus. What do you see, hear, smell, and feel?"

Several hands shot up, and Ms. Lopez nodded to Liam. "I think I'll see a lot of colors everywhere," he said thoughtfully. "Like bright flags and costumes, maybe even decorations we've never seen before."

Ms. Lopez smiled. "Great guess, Liam! Festivals are often full of color, especially ones that celebrate different cultures."

Mia raised her hand next. "I think I'll smell different foods cooking," she said. "Maybe things we haven't tried before, like new spices."

"Absolutely," Ms. Lopez agreed. "Food is a big part of culture, and we might encounter flavors and smells that are new to us. And remember, we don't have to like everything, but it's fun to try."

Ethan, ever the bold one, added, "I bet we'll hear some awesome music. Like drums and maybe even instruments we don't know. I love listening to different kinds of music."

"Good thinking, Ethan!" Ms. Lopez said. "Music can tell us so much about a culture. Sometimes, instruments and rhythms are passed down through generations, so they carry a lot of history and tradition."

The students kept guessing, painting a mental picture of the festival through their imaginations. With each guess, the excitement built until it felt like the air on the bus was buzzing with energy. Even the quieter students were leaning forward, caught up in the enthusiasm of the moment. Each child's idea added another layer to their shared vision of the festival, bringing them closer together as a group.

Then, Ms. Lopez suggested a different activity. "Let's each say one thing we're most excited to see or learn today. It can be anything—a type of music, food, art, or a new word in a different language."

She began, sharing that she was looking forward to learning about different forms of dance. "Dance is a way people share joy and tell stories, and I'm excited to see what stories we might uncover," she said.

One by one, each student shared their own hopes and dreams for the day. Mia was excited about seeing traditional clothing, Emma was curious about trying new foods, and Jackson couldn't wait to see the different kinds of art. When they finished, each student had voiced their own unique wish for the day, creating a sense of shared purpose and unity.

As the bus rolled along, Ms. Lopez handed out small booklets with pictures and descriptions of some of the things they might encounter at the festival—art, instruments, food, clothing, and symbols. She encouraged the students to look through the booklets and to take note of anything that looked interesting or unfamiliar. It was like a little preview of the festival, sparking even more questions and guesses.

Chapter 4: First Impressions

The bus slowed to a stop, and a hush fell over Ms. Lopez's class as they craned their necks to catch their first glimpse of the multicultural festival. Through the large bus windows, the students saw vibrant banners fluttering in the breeze, decorated with colors and patterns unlike anything they'd seen before. People of all ages milled about, many wearing outfits that sparkled with beads, shimmered with fabric, or flowed in brilliant hues of red, blue, yellow, and green. The air seemed to buzz with excitement, and from where they sat, they could hear faint music playing—a combination of drums, flutes, and voices in harmonious song.

Ms. Lopez stood up at the front of the bus. "Alright, everyone! This is it—our big adventure!" she said with a smile. "Before we step off the bus, let's remember the three words we talked about all week: Respect, Curiosity, and Open-mindedness. Today, we're guests in a place filled with traditions, stories, and experiences that are new to us. So, let's do our best to listen, learn, and appreciate everything we see."

The students nodded eagerly. Each one of them was ready, some practically bouncing in their seats with excitement. As they filed off the bus, Ms. Lopez handed each student a small wristband with the word "Explorer" written on it, symbolizing that they were there to explore, discover, and learn.

Stepping out onto the festival grounds felt like walking into a whole new world. The air was thick with the smells of spices, roasted nuts, and sweet pastries from nearby food stalls. Around them, people spoke in different languages, some familiar and others completely new. There were tents set up in neat rows, each decorated with flags, traditional items, or posters featuring photographs and stories. From the first moment, Ms. Lopez could see that her students were captivated, their eyes darting from one vibrant display to another.

As they walked, they were greeted by a friendly festival guide named Mr. Ray. He was an older man with a kind face and a broad smile, dressed in a loose tunic with intricate embroidery. "Welcome, students of Riverside Elementary!" he said warmly, his voice full of joy. "Today, you'll journey through different worlds, each filled with music, stories, and traditions that people have cherished for generations. I'll be here to help answer questions, share stories, and guide you through your explorations. I hope you're ready for a memorable adventure!"

The students gave him enthusiastic nods and murmurs of "yes" and "we can't wait!" Mr. Ray's warm welcome immediately made them feel at ease, even those who were feeling a bit shy or nervous. It was clear that he loved sharing the festival's wonders with young learners, and that enthusiasm was contagious.

Mr. Ray began leading them toward the first tent, which was adorned with hanging lanterns in shades of gold, orange, and crimson. As they approached, they could see rows of beautiful art on display: paintings, sculptures, and textiles, each piece telling a story. Mr. Ray explained that this tent was dedicated to traditional art forms, a way for people to express their histories, beliefs, and dreams through colors, patterns, and shapes.

The students fanned out, moving from one display to the next, their eyes widening as they took in each detail. Some pieces were bold and vibrant, depicting animals, landscapes, and everyday life, while others were delicate and intricate, with patterns so fine it was hard to imagine the patience and skill they required. Ms. Lopez encouraged her students to take notes or sketch their favorite pieces, reminding them that art could tell a story without using any words at all.

Mia was drawn to a painting of a sun rising over a mountain range. The colors seemed to leap off the canvas, swirling together in shades of pink, orange, and gold. She could almost feel the warmth of the sun and the calm of the morning captured in the strokes of the brush. "I wonder what this picture means to the artist," she said aloud, mostly to herself.

Mr. Ray, overhearing her, walked over. "That's a beautiful question, Mia," he said, smiling. "In many cultures, the sun represents new beginnings, hope, and strength. It's a symbol of resilience and renewal."

Mia nodded, suddenly understanding the painting on a deeper level. She scribbled a few words in her notebook: "The sun means hope. Art can show feelings without words." She felt proud of her new insight, feeling like a true explorer of ideas and symbols.

A few tents down, Ethan and Jackson were mesmerized by a wall covered in masks, each one carved and painted with distinct colors and shapes. Mr. Ray explained that in some traditions, masks were worn during ceremonies or festivals to honor ancestors, represent spirits, or tell stories through dance. Ethan pointed to a mask that had fierce eyes and sharp, bold colors, remarking, "This one looks like it's alive!"

Mr. Ray chuckled. "You're not the only one who thinks that. Masks are powerful symbols. They're often crafted to represent the qualities or traits that people admire or even fear."

Jackson leaned closer, carefully sketching the mask in his notebook. "I feel like I can see a story just by looking at it," he said, amazed by the mask's expressive features. He made a note to himself to ask more about the meaning of each design.

As they left the art tent, the group followed the sounds of drums and bells, coming from a circle of musicians who were gathered under a canopy. People sat around them, clapping along and swaying to the beat. The students joined the crowd, captivated by the rhythm and energy of the music. The musicians were playing an assortment of instruments—some familiar, like drums and tambourines, and others completely new, like a long flute carved with swirling patterns.

Mr. Ray explained that each instrument had its own story. "Some of these instruments have been passed down through generations, and each one carries the spirit of those who played it before," he said.

"Music is a way people communicate feelings, tell stories, and come together. Even if you don't speak the same language, you can still share a song."

Ethan couldn't help but tap his foot to the beat, and soon a few students were clapping along with the rhythm. The musicians, noticing the enthusiastic audience, invited the students to join them in a simple clapping pattern. The students laughed as they tried to keep up, some missing the beat but enjoying themselves thoroughly.

Chapter 5: Exploring the Art Pavilion

After a lunch break filled with excited chatter and stories of what they'd seen so far, Ms. Lopez's class regrouped, ready for the next part of their journey. With full stomachs and fresh energy, they followed their guide, Mr. Ray, toward one of the festival's largest tents: the Art Pavilion. The tent was enormous, its canopy decorated with swirling designs and draped fabrics in every color of the rainbow. From a distance, the students could already see beautiful displays of art peeking out from within—paintings, sculptures, textiles, and intricate pieces that seemed to tell stories of their own. This was not just a tent; it was a world filled with imagination, tradition, and expression.

As they stepped inside, the students gasped. The pavilion was filled with light, color, and texture in every direction. Art pieces were arranged in carefully organized sections, each display grouped by a particular theme or style. There were areas dedicated to sculptures, to paintings, and to fabric arts like weaving and embroidery. Each section seemed to radiate its own unique character, reflecting different cultural styles and techniques.

Mr. Ray paused at the entrance, letting the students take in the sights. "Welcome to the Art Pavilion," he said with a smile. "Here, you'll see how people from around the world express themselves, their beliefs, and their stories through art. Every piece you see here has a meaning, a purpose, and a story behind it. Today, you'll get a chance to create your own art, inspired by what you see, and learn a few techniques along the way."

Ms. Lopez encouraged the students to spread out and explore, reminding them to be respectful and to take notes or make sketches of anything that inspired them. Mia was one of the first to move forward, her eyes already darting from one display to the next. She was drawn to a section filled with textiles—beautiful, intricate pieces woven with vibrant colors and complex patterns.

As she approached, she noticed an elderly woman seated behind a loom, her hands deftly working threads in and out, creating patterns as if by magic. Mia watched, mesmerized by the woman's focus and skill. The woman smiled at her, gesturing for her to come closer. "This is weaving," the woman explained kindly, her voice soft yet full of pride. "It's a tradition in my family that goes back many generations. Each pattern has a meaning; some represent the mountains, others the rivers, and some even tell the stories of my ancestors."

Mia was captivated. She had never thought of art as something that could hold memories, places, and people within it. She watched the woman's hands as they moved expertly, almost hypnotically, and she could almost feel the centuries of tradition woven into each thread. Inspired, she pulled out her notebook and sketched a few of the patterns, making notes about what the woman had told her. She wanted to remember every detail.

Meanwhile, Jackson found himself in front of a display of clay sculptures, each piece so detailed that he felt as though they were alive. The sculptures depicted animals, people, and scenes of everyday life. Some were small and delicate, while others were bold and expressive. He reached out to touch one of the pieces, but stopped himself, remembering the importance of respect. Instead, he turned to Mr. Ray, who had joined him, curious about the sculptures' meaning.

"These sculptures are made with clay, a material from the earth," Mr. Ray explained. "For many people, clay represents a connection to the land, to nature. By shaping it into these figures, the artists give life to their beliefs, their stories, and the creatures that share their world."

Jackson nodded, fascinated by the idea. He thought about how a simple material like clay could be transformed into something meaningful, something that could tell a story. As he looked at the details in the sculptures—the eyes, the shapes of the hands, the expressions on the animals' faces—he realized that each piece was unique, carrying the artist's perspective and imagination within it.

Inspired, he made a note to try working with clay when he got home, eager to see what stories he could shape.

Emma, on the other hand, was drawn to a section filled with paintings. Some were abstract, with bold splashes of color and unusual shapes, while others depicted peaceful landscapes or moments of celebration. One painting, in particular, caught her attention. It showed a family gathered around a large table, sharing a meal under the stars. The colors were warm and inviting, and she could almost feel the laughter and warmth of the gathering.

Mr. Ray noticed her interest and approached, explaining that the painting represented family, togetherness, and gratitude. "In many cultures," he said, "sharing a meal is more than just eating food. It's a way to bond, to celebrate, and to show love for one another."

Emma nodded thoughtfully. She'd never considered that a painting could capture something so deeply emotional and universal. In her notebook, she wrote, "Art can show family and love." She felt a new sense of connection, realizing that people all over the world found ways to express love and gratitude in their own special ways.

Ethan, ever curious, found himself in front of a section showcasing masks, each one more fascinating than the last. Some were decorated with feathers, others with beads, and a few were even painted in bright, contrasting colors. Each mask seemed to hold a different personality, as if it were alive with stories waiting to be told. Ethan remembered the masks he had seen earlier in the festival and wondered if these were used in similar ways.

Mr. Ray explained that masks are often worn during ceremonies or dances, each one representing a character or spirit. "Masks have power," he said. "They can transform the person who wears them, allowing them to embody a different spirit, a different energy."

Ethan was entranced. He imagined himself wearing one of the masks, feeling the weight and texture on his face, and transforming into someone—or something—else. He jotted down a few notes in his notebook, scribbling, "Masks can change who you are." He felt a thrill of excitement, as though he had been let in on a secret that was both mysterious and powerful.

Sophia wandered over to a section where large fabric tapestries hung from the walls, each one embroidered with intricate patterns and symbols. She admired the bright colors and the way the patterns seemed to tell a story, even if she couldn't understand what it meant. A woman standing nearby explained that these tapestries were often used to mark special occasions, like weddings or festivals, and that each symbol represented something important—a bird for freedom, a flower for beauty, or a river for life.

Chapter 6: Music Workshop – Rhythms and Beats

After their time in the Art Pavilion, Ms. Lopez's students were energized and inspired, each carrying a piece of art they had made with pride. But before they could rest too long, Mr. Ray appeared, clapping his hands to gather their attention. "Alright, young explorers! Our next stop is just around the corner, and I have a feeling you're going to enjoy it," he said, his eyes twinkling with excitement. "We're heading to the Music Workshop!"

The students let out excited murmurs, and a few even gave cheers. They had heard the sounds of drums, flutes, and bells in the distance since they arrived, and now they were finally going to see where that beautiful music was coming from. They followed Mr. Ray across the festival grounds, weaving through groups of festival-goers and booths filled with trinkets and colorful clothing.

As they rounded a corner, the sounds of rhythmic drumming grew louder, filling the air with an infectious beat. They approached a large open tent decorated with strings of colorful ribbons and hanging wind chimes that clinked gently in the breeze. Inside, a group of musicians was gathered, each playing an instrument unique to their culture. Some of the instruments were familiar, like drums and guitars, while others were new and mysterious, like a tall stringed instrument with a soft, melodic tone and a set of carved wooden blocks that produced a rich, hollow sound when struck.

The musicians paused as the students entered, offering warm smiles and nods of welcome. One of them, a man with a long beard and a joyful expression, stepped forward and introduced himself as Samir. "Hello, young friends! Welcome to the world of rhythm and beats!" he said, gesturing to the instruments around him. "Today, we're going to take a journey through music. We'll teach you how rhythm connects us, and you'll even get a chance to make some music of your own."

The students listened, their eyes wide with anticipation. They were fascinated by the variety of instruments before them, each one hinting at stories and sounds they had never heard. Ms. Lopez encouraged them to keep an open mind and to remember that, just like with the art they had seen, music was a way for people to express themselves and connect with one another.

Samir began by introducing them to each instrument, taking his time to explain where it came from, what it was made of, and how it was used. He started with a drum made from wood and animal skin. "This is a djembe," he explained, his hands resting on the drum. "It comes from a tradition where people gather in circles to play music together. The djembe's rhythm is powerful—it can carry messages and set the pace for dances."

He struck the drum with his hands, and the deep, resonant sound filled the tent. The students felt the vibration in their chests, each beat creating a pulse that seemed to connect them all. They couldn't help but move their feet or tap their fingers along with the rhythm, drawn to the drum's steady and compelling beat.

Next, Samir introduced them to a stringed instrument called the sitar. It was long and slender, with a beautiful carved neck and delicate strings stretched across its body. "This is a sitar, an instrument that has been used for centuries to tell stories through music," Samir said, plucking a string and letting the note linger in the air. The sound was soft, like a whisper that filled the room with mystery and emotion.

The students were captivated, leaning forward to catch every note. Emma whispered to Mia, "It sounds like the music is telling a secret."

Samir smiled, as if he had overheard her. "In many cultures, music is indeed a way to share stories and secrets, to express feelings that words cannot capture. The sitar is used to create melodies that touch the heart, and its sound is said to bring peace and calm."

He then moved on to a set of small drums called bongos, which were paired with a series of wooden percussion blocks. "These are used to create rhythm patterns that are light and playful. You'll find them in festivals, celebrations, and gatherings where people come together to dance and celebrate," Samir explained, tapping out a quick, lively rhythm that made the students smile.

After he introduced the different instruments, Samir invited each student to choose an instrument to play. The students scattered, eagerly picking up drums, bells, and wooden clappers. Samir guided them through some basic rhythms, encouraging them to listen carefully to each other and to the beat he was setting. "Listen to the rhythm around you," he said, "and feel how each beat fits with the others. Music is about more than just making noise—it's about creating harmony, a sound that brings people together."

Ethan, holding a djembe, began experimenting with its deep, resonant sound. He tapped the drum with his fingers, feeling the vibration and enjoying the powerful notes it produced. Beside him, Sophia held a small set of handbells. She shook them gently, adding a soft, melodic layer to Ethan's steady beat. The two grinned at each other, excited by the way their instruments blended together.

Ms. Lopez observed with pride as her students tried different rhythms, each one adding their unique sound to the mix. Some were shy at first, tapping hesitantly, while others, like Ethan, dived in with enthusiasm, playing confidently and even trying new patterns. She watched as the students listened to each other, adjusting their playing to match the rhythm Samir was setting. It was beautiful to see how quickly they learned to work together, finding their places within the rhythm.

As the students became more comfortable, Samir guided them in creating a simple rhythm circle. "Music is like a heartbeat," he explained. "Each beat is a part of a larger pattern, and each sound has its place. When we play together, we create something bigger than ourselves. We create a rhythm that connects us all."

The students began playing in unison, following the rhythm Samir set. Some beat their drums slowly, others added quick taps or shakes with bells, and a few students with clappers kept a steady beat. Slowly, the music grew, filling the tent with sound. They weren't just playing individually anymore; they were part of a collective rhythm, each student's sound blending into the whole.

At one point, Mia closed her eyes, feeling the beat more deeply. She let herself get lost in the rhythm, sensing how her hands moved in sync with the others. It felt like she was part of something ancient and important, as if she were connected not only to her classmates but to all the people who had ever played music together. When she opened her eyes, she saw that her classmates were smiling and tapping their feet, immersed in the same experience.

Chapter 7: Stories from the Heart

After leaving the Music Workshop, Ms. Lopez's class gathered under a large tree with wide branches that stretched out like a welcoming embrace. The afternoon sun cast dappled shadows on the ground, creating a soft, calming atmosphere. The students sat on colorful mats, still humming to themselves or tapping soft rhythms on their knees, the music they'd created lingering like a melody in their minds. Ms. Lopez could see how the music had stirred something special within them—a deeper sense of connection and understanding. But now it was time for something different, something that would take them into a world of imagination, lessons, and timeless tales.

As the students settled down, they noticed an older woman approaching. She had long, silver hair braided over one shoulder, and she wore a flowing robe decorated with embroidered symbols that seemed to tell stories of their own. She moved gracefully, and her eyes sparkled as though she knew many secrets. Her face was warm and welcoming, and as she sat down, she looked at each child, as if silently inviting them to join her in a shared journey.

"Hello, young friends," she greeted them in a voice that was both soft and strong, carrying a timeless quality that instantly captivated them. "My name is Kira, and today, I will be sharing with you some stories from the heart. These are stories that have traveled across many lands and through many generations. They've been told under starry skies, beside glowing fires, and in the warm embrace of family gatherings. Today, I am honored to share them with you."

The students leaned in, entranced by her words and the magic in her voice. There was a stillness in the air, as though the world itself was holding its breath, waiting for the stories to begin. Kira took a deep breath, her gaze sweeping over the group, and then she began her first tale.

The story was of a brave and clever young girl named Layla, who lived in a village surrounded by tall mountains. One winter, her village faced a terrible drought, and the rivers dried up. Layla's family, like many others, struggled to find enough water to survive. Despite her small size and young age, Layla was determined to help her people. She traveled deep into the mountains, guided by stories her grandmother had told her of a hidden spring that only the truly brave could find. Along her journey, Layla faced many challenges—a fierce wind that tried to blow her back, steep cliffs, and even her own fear. But each time, she remembered her family and her village, and she pressed on.

As Kira spoke, her voice took on the strength and courage of young Layla, and the students could almost see the mountains, feel the icy wind, and sense Layla's determination. Finally, Layla found the hidden spring, and with her hands cupped, she brought water back to her village. Her courage and selflessness saved her people, and from that day on, she was remembered as a hero.

When Kira finished, a hush fell over the group. The story had transported them, showing them a world where bravery could be found in the smallest of hearts. Ms. Lopez noticed that Mia had a tear in her eye, her expression one of awe. Mia whispered to herself, "I want to be brave like Layla." She wrote down a note in her notebook, "Bravery can come in small sizes," as if to remember this lesson forever.

Kira allowed a moment for the story to settle, for the images and lessons to find their places in each child's heart. Then, she began her next story, a tale of a kind and gentle lion named Nuru who lived in a lush, green forest. Nuru was known as the strongest and mightiest animal in the forest, but he was also known for his kindness. One day, the forest was threatened by a fierce fire. Many animals were scared and unsure of where to go, and even though Nuru could have saved himself by running to the river, he chose to stay and help. He guided the smaller animals to safety, using his strength to protect them from the flames and his gentle voice to calm their fears.

The students listened, their eyes wide, as Kira described Nuru's bravery and selflessness. They could almost hear the crackling fire, see the frightened faces of the animals, and feel the strength in Nuru's heart. It was a story that celebrated kindness as the truest form of strength, teaching them that real heroes were those who cared for others.

Jackson, who usually thought of strength in terms of muscles and loud voices, felt a new understanding bloom within him. He realized that being strong didn't always mean being the biggest or the toughest. Sometimes, it meant having the heart to help others, even when it was hard. He wrote in his notebook, "Kindness is strength," and underlined it, feeling as though he had discovered something important about himself.

As Kira continued to share her stories, each one brought a new lesson, a new perspective. She told of clever foxes who used their wits to solve problems, of wise old turtles who taught patience and persistence, and of families who loved each other despite all odds. Each tale was filled with characters who were flawed yet admirable, faced with challenges that seemed insurmountable but who found a way to overcome them through resilience, compassion, or intelligence.

One of the students, Liam, was particularly drawn to a story about a family of birds who built their nest on the edge of a cliff. Every year, storms would come, and each time, the family would rebuild their nest with patience and care, never giving up despite the constant hardships. Through Kira's words, Liam saw the power of perseverance, realizing that strength was not always about winning but about having the courage to try again and again.

Ms. Lopez observed her students, seeing how each story touched them in a unique way. She watched as they jotted down notes, some writing words like "bravery," "kindness," and "family" in big, bold letters, while others drew little sketches inspired by the characters and events in Kira's stories. It was as though each story had planted a seed, and she could see the beginnings of growth, understanding, and empathy sprouting within each child.

As Kira shared her final story, the atmosphere was one of deep respect and stillness. This last tale was a fable about a river and a mountain, two friends who often quarreled. The mountain, tall and proud, would mock the river for being so low and winding, while the river would tease the mountain for being rigid and unchanging. One day, a fierce storm came, and the mountain, strong as it was, began to crumble. The river, however, remained resilient, winding its way through the valleys and carrying the mountain's broken stones with it, supporting and softening its friend. Through this story, Kira taught that both strength and flexibility were valuable, and that sometimes, true strength lay in being adaptable and kind.

Chapter 8: Dance of Joy

With hearts full from the stories they had heard, Ms. Lopez's class followed Mr. Ray to the next part of their festival journey. They could hear music playing in the distance, faint at first but growing louder and more energetic with each step. Drums, flutes, and voices blended into a lively rhythm, filling the air with an undeniable sense of celebration and movement. The students, already in high spirits from Kira's storytelling, found their steps quickening in anticipation. There was something about the beat, the way it pulsed and flowed, that made them feel light and excited.

Finally, they arrived at a large, open area covered with smooth, polished wood flooring. A stage was set up at one end, decorated with bright tapestries, flowers, and ribbons in every color imaginable. Performers stood on stage, dressed in traditional outfits that shimmered and swayed with their movements, each garment carefully crafted and full of life. The dancers moved gracefully in time to the music, their feet light on the floor, their arms sweeping through the air in unison. They spun, clapped, and jumped, moving in ways that seemed both effortless and deeply meaningful. Their faces shone with joy, as if each step and gesture were a celebration of something larger than words.

Ms. Lopez's students watched, transfixed by the beauty and energy of the dance. Some of them had never seen anything like it before, and they couldn't help but sway to the beat. Even the shyest among them, who might have felt self-conscious about dancing in public, found themselves tapping their toes or nodding their heads. The rhythm was infectious, and soon the whole class seemed to be moving along, carried away by the spirit of the dance.

After the performance, the dancers bowed to the audience, their faces glowing from exertion and joy. The crowd erupted in applause, and Ms. Lopez's students clapped with enthusiasm, some of them even cheering out loud. The dancers smiled and waved, clearly pleased to have shared their tradition with such an appreciative audience. As the applause faded, one of the dancers stepped forward and addressed the crowd, her voice warm and inviting.

"Hello, everyone! My name is Aisha, and I'm so happy you could join us today," she said, smiling. "Dancing is a way for us to express joy, to celebrate life, and to connect with each other. We believe that when we dance, we're sharing not just our movements, but our stories, our history, and our hearts."

She looked around at the crowd, her eyes landing on Ms. Lopez's students. "Would you like to join us in learning a dance?" she asked, her smile widening as the children's faces lit up with excitement.

The students turned to Ms. Lopez, their eyes wide with anticipation. Ms. Lopez nodded encouragingly. "Go ahead, everyone! This is your chance to learn something new, to step out of your comfort zones, and to feel the music in a whole new way."

With a chorus of excited cheers, the students hurried to join Aisha and her fellow dancers on the dance floor. The performers formed a large circle, inviting the children to join hands with them, linking everyone together. The students reached out, some of them hesitantly, others boldly, until they were all connected. It was a powerful feeling, standing there in a circle, holding hands with people from different backgrounds, all there to share a moment of joy and unity.

Aisha explained that they would start with some basic steps, teaching the students a traditional dance that was both simple and meaningful. She demonstrated the first step, lifting her foot and bringing it down gently in time to the beat. The students watched closely, some of them practicing the movement on their own before joining in. The music began softly, a steady beat that matched the rhythm of the dance.

"Just feel the music," Aisha encouraged them. "Let it guide your movements. This dance is not about being perfect; it's about celebrating the moment, being together, and letting yourself be free."

The students followed her lead, some a little clumsily at first, but soon they began to find the rhythm. They moved their feet in time with the beat, lifting and stepping, lifting and stepping, until the entire circle moved as one. Aisha showed them how to add a clap between steps, and soon the sound of hands clapping filled the air, blending with the beat of the drums. The students laughed, the awkwardness melting away as they lost themselves in the dance.

Emma, who was usually quiet and reserved, found herself smiling broadly, her feet moving naturally to the rhythm. She felt light, as if the music had lifted her spirit, freeing her from the worries and doubts she usually held inside. She glanced around and saw her friends, each one moving joyfully, their faces alight with the same happiness she felt.

Ethan, who was full of energy and often a little mischievous, embraced the dance with enthusiasm. He added extra hops and claps, his movements big and bold, filling the space with his personality. For him, the dance was an opportunity to express himself in a way that felt natural and fun. He noticed that even Ms. Lopez was swaying along at the edge of the circle, her eyes sparkling as she watched her students embrace the moment.

After a few rounds of the basic steps, Aisha introduced a more intricate movement. She showed them how to spin, keeping their balance as they twirled and then returning to their place in the circle. The students watched closely, eager to try, and soon they were spinning in time to the music, laughing as they twirled back into place. A few stumbled and giggled, catching themselves before they fell, but they didn't mind. The dance was full of joy, and mistakes only made them laugh harder.

As the music grew faster, Aisha encouraged them to let go and move however they felt. "Dancing is about expressing yourself," she said, her voice rising over the music. "Let your movements be your own. Show us your joy, your excitement, and your energy!"

With her encouragement, the students began to add their own twists to the dance. Some moved faster, others slower, but each one danced in their own way, letting their personalities shine through. It was a beautiful sight, each child expressing themselves, yet remaining part of the group, moving to the same beat. They weren't just learning steps; they were learning to trust their bodies, to find joy in movement, and to connect with others through shared experience.

After a while, Aisha gathered everyone in a close circle and taught them a special part of the dance, a movement that represented gratitude. They placed their hands over their hearts, then lifted them toward the sky, as if offering thanks. She explained that in her culture, dancing was a way of giving thanks for the beauty of life, for family, for friends, and for moments of joy. This part of the dance was a reminder to appreciate all the gifts in life, big and small.

The students performed the movement together, hands on their hearts, then reaching toward the sky. It was a solemn moment, and even the most playful students, like Ethan, took it seriously, feeling the weight of the gesture. Ms. Lopez watched, her heart full as she saw her students embracing this moment of gratitude and reflection. She knew this experience was giving them a new way to express appreciation, to understand that joy and thankfulness could be celebrated through movement as well as words.

When the music finally slowed and came to a gentle end, the students were breathless, their faces flushed, but their spirits lifted. They clapped for Aisha and the other dancers, thanking them for the experience. Aisha smiled warmly, bowing slightly. "Thank you, each of you, for dancing with us. Remember, dancing is more than just steps and movements. It's a way to share joy, to tell a story, and to connect with others. I hope you carry this joy with you, and that you continue to dance in your own way."

As the students gathered to leave, they talked excitedly among themselves, sharing their favorite parts of the dance and comparing the little moves they had added to make it their own. Some even tried to recreate the steps, laughing as they stumbled and spun around. It was clear that the experience had given them something special—a freedom to express themselves, to feel joy without restraint, and to celebrate life with open hearts.

Ms. Lopez walked with them, her own heart light from watching her students experience such pure happiness. She knew that the dance had taught them more than any lesson in a classroom could. It had shown them the beauty of sharing joy, of moving with others in harmony, and of letting go of fear or self-consciousness. She saw how the dance had brought out qualities in each student—confidence, creativity, openness—that would stay with them long after the festival ended.

Chapter 9: Trying on Traditional Clothing

After the dance session, Ms. Lopez gathered her students once again, each one still buzzing with excitement and joy from their experience. Their faces were flushed, and they were all talking at once, trying to describe the moments that had made them feel the happiest or the freest. As they made their way through the festival grounds, their attention was caught by a large, colorful tent draped in fabrics of every color and texture. Patterns of intricate designs adorned the entrance, drawing them in with their vivid colors and the promise of something magical waiting inside.

Mr. Ray gestured to the tent with a warm smile. "Our next adventure is one of transformation," he said. "Inside this tent, you'll get a chance to try on traditional clothing from cultures around the world. These clothes tell stories of their own—stories of history, climate, craftsmanship, and even beliefs. Each garment is a piece of art, crafted carefully and worn with pride. Clothes, like language and dance, are a way to express identity and tradition."

The students exchanged curious glances, intrigued by the idea of trying on clothing that held such deep significance. Most of them had never thought much about what clothing could represent beyond fashion and style. But as they entered the tent, they were struck by the incredible variety and beauty of the clothes displayed. Each garment seemed to speak a language of its own, vibrant with meaning.

Inside, rows of racks displayed outfits from different cultures, each with unique patterns, colors, and textures. Some garments were decorated with bold embroidery, while others were woven with delicate threads in subtle hues. There were long robes, flowing dresses, jackets with intricate stitching, hats, scarves, and even shoes that looked like they'd been crafted with painstaking attention to detail. The entire space was a kaleidoscope of colors and designs, a tribute to the diversity of human expression.

A friendly woman named Leena greeted them. She wore a dress that flowed to the ground, decorated with symbols and motifs that seemed to tell a story of their own. She smiled warmly at the students and invited them to explore the clothing, encouraging them to touch the fabrics, feel the textures, and admire the details.

"Every piece you see here is special," Leena explained. "They're not just clothes; they're expressions of culture, climate, history, and creativity. In some places, clothes are designed to keep people cool in the hot sun, while in other places, they are meant to keep people warm during the freezing winters. Some of these garments are worn for celebrations, others for ceremonies, and some are worn every day with pride."

The students moved slowly around the room, taking in the incredible variety before them. Mia ran her fingers over a delicate shawl woven with tiny golden threads, mesmerized by the way it shimmered in the light. She could imagine someone wearing it for a special occasion, surrounded by family and friends, the golden threads catching the light as they moved.

Ethan found himself drawn to a thick, woolen jacket decorated with bright embroidery and tiny bells sewn into the seams. The jacket was heavy in his hands, and he could tell it was made to keep someone warm in a place where winters were fierce. He thought about the people who might wear such a jacket, trudging through snow-covered landscapes, and he felt a new respect for how clothes could be both beautiful and practical.

Jackson was fascinated by a brightly colored outfit with geometric patterns that covered the entire fabric. He noticed that the patterns repeated in a way that felt almost musical, like a rhythm woven into the cloth. He asked Leena about it, and she explained that some cultures use patterns to tell stories or to represent important symbols like mountains, rivers, or animals. The thought of clothing as a canvas for storytelling opened up a new world for Jackson, who scribbled in his notebook, "Patterns are like stories in clothes."

One by one, the students chose pieces to try on, carefully selecting items that drew them in. Leena and her assistants helped them put on the garments, adjusting scarves, tying sashes, and explaining the significance of each item. The students looked at themselves in mirrors, laughing as they admired their transformations. Each garment seemed to change not just their appearance but their posture, making them stand a little taller, as though they were trying to live up to the importance of the clothes they were wearing.

Emma chose a long dress with flowing sleeves and intricate embroidery. The fabric was light and airy, and the colors reminded her of a sunset, with shades of orange, pink, and purple blending together in a soft gradient. She felt elegant and graceful, as though she were dressed for a festival or a ceremony. The embroidery told a story, and Leena explained that each color and shape represented something—a flower for beauty, a star for dreams, and a wave for the strength to overcome challenges.

Emma couldn't stop smiling as she twirled, watching the dress billow around her. She realized that the person who wore this dress was not just showing off beauty but was surrounded by symbols of hope, dreams, and resilience. In her notebook, she wrote, "Clothes can hold dreams and stories," wanting to remember the feeling that had filled her as she wore the dress.

Liam, who often preferred simple clothes, chose a long robe with intricate designs along the edges. It was a deep shade of blue, with golden threads woven into patterns that reminded him of the night sky. As he put it on, he felt calm and dignified, as though the robe were helping him connect to something bigger than himself. He learned that in some cultures, dark colors and gold are used to represent wisdom and strength, symbols of knowledge and guidance.

As he stood in front of the mirror, he felt a quiet confidence settle over him. He thought about the people who wore this type of robe, imagining wise elders or storytellers who shared knowledge with their communities. For the first time, he felt as though clothes could be something powerful, a symbol of respect and wisdom.

Ethan, always full of energy, chose a garment decorated with bright colors and layers of fabric that looked festive and lively. Leena explained that this type of clothing was often worn during celebrations, where people danced, sang, and laughed together. Ethan felt immediately at home in the outfit, spinning around and laughing as the layers swirled around him.

"People who wear this must have so much fun!" he said, beaming.

Leena nodded, smiling. "Exactly. In some places, bright colors are used to celebrate joy, life, and community. When you wear these colors, you're showing that you're happy to be part of the celebration, that you're full of life."

Ethan scribbled down a note, "Clothes can show happiness," wanting to remember that feeling. He felt like he understood something new about celebration and expression, how clothes could be a way to show the world how you felt on the inside.

Sophia, drawn to soft fabrics, chose a delicate scarf embroidered with tiny flowers. Leena explained that this scarf was made to honor nature, each flower representing a different season. Sophia wrapped it around her shoulders, feeling as though she were wearing a piece of a garden. She realized that clothing could be a way to bring a piece of nature close, even for people who lived far from fields and flowers.

Chapter 10: Learning New Languages

The afternoon sun cast a warm glow over the festival as Ms. Lopez's class gathered near the Language Tent. After a day filled with dancing, stories, art, and traditional clothing, the students were both exhilarated and a little tired. Still, the sight of the Language Tent, with its banners and signs displaying words and phrases from different languages, renewed their excitement. The tent was inviting, draped with colorful fabrics printed with symbols and letters that were unfamiliar yet intriguing. Each sign was a reminder of the countless languages spoken around the world, each carrying its own beauty, rhythm, and expression.

Ms. Lopez gathered her students in a circle just outside the tent and reminded them to keep open minds and curious hearts. She explained that learning even a few words in another language could create connections that went beyond borders and differences. She could see their eyes shining with anticipation, ready to dive into the world of language.

Inside the tent, tables were arranged in a semicircle, each one dedicated to a different language and guided by a native speaker eager to share their language and culture. Some tables displayed letters written in intricate scripts, while others showed symbols and sounds unfamiliar to the students. It was a colorful, vibrant world within the tent, filled with people ready to share their words, their stories, and their greetings.

A woman named Ana, with a warm smile and a gentle demeanor, approached the group. "Welcome to the Language Tent!" she greeted them. "Today, you'll have a chance to learn words and phrases from all over the world. Languages are like bridges, connecting people and helping them understand each other. A simple greeting, a thank you, or a goodbye in another language can open doors to friendship and understanding."

The students listened, captivated by Ana's words. They hadn't thought of languages as bridges before, but now the idea filled them with curiosity. Ana explained that each student would have the chance to move from table to table, learning a few basic phrases from each language. She encouraged them to ask questions, repeat the words, and practice with one another.

The first table they visited was hosted by a man named Omar, who spoke with a rhythmic, musical voice that captured the students' attention. He introduced a few basic phrases for greeting someone, like "hello" and "thank you." The students repeated after him, a little shyly at first but gaining confidence with each attempt. Omar explained that in his culture, greeting someone properly was a way to show respect and warmth, a way to say, "I see you, and I welcome you."

Emma, usually soft-spoken, felt herself smiling as she repeated the greeting, hearing how her voice took on a new rhythm and cadence. The sound of the unfamiliar words felt strange on her tongue, but also thrilling. She realized that learning these words was like unlocking a secret, a way to connect with someone who might otherwise be a stranger. In her notebook, she wrote, "Words make friends," wanting to remember this moment of discovery.

Moving on, the students gathered around a table where a young woman named Yuki taught them a few words in her language. She showed them how to say "please" and "thank you," explaining that these words were often accompanied by small gestures of politeness, like a slight bow of the head. She demonstrated, and the students mimicked her movements, feeling how the gestures gave weight and meaning to the words. Yuki explained that these gestures showed humility and gratitude, values that her culture cherished deeply.

Ethan tried the words with enthusiasm, enjoying the rhythm and sound, but he struggled a bit with the bow. Yuki laughed gently and reassured him that it was okay to feel awkward. "Respect isn't always about getting it perfect," she said, her voice kind. "It's about the intention behind your actions." Ethan felt a warmth in her words, realizing that trying was what mattered most. He scribbled in his notebook, "Respect is in the effort," feeling proud of his newfound understanding.

At the next table, they met a man named Carlos, who introduced them to his language's word for "family." He explained that family was deeply important in his culture, and the word itself carried a sense of warmth, closeness, and love. Carlos shared that in his culture, people often used family terms like "aunt," "uncle," or "brother" for close friends, extending their family circle beyond blood relations. The students were intrigued, surprised that words could expand the meaning of family and make a community feel more united.

Jackson, who had never thought of family as something so flexible, felt moved by this idea. The thought that family could include friends, neighbors, and community members filled him with a sense of belonging. He wrote in his notebook, "Family can be anyone you love," realizing that family was less about who you were related to and more about who cared for you.

As they continued exploring, the students came across a table where an older woman named Zara taught them phrases related to nature. She showed them the word for "river" and explained that in her language, this word was used not only to describe the water itself but also as a symbol for life and continuity. She shared that in her culture, rivers were seen as sacred, as they provided water, carried stories, and connected villages.

Sophia, who loved nature, was fascinated by this idea. She repeated the word for river, feeling the reverence in Zara's voice. She realized that words could carry meaning beyond their literal definitions, connecting people to the land and each other. In her notebook, she wrote, "Words are part of nature," feeling as if she had gained a new respect for the power of language.

Chapter 11: Tasting Flavors from Around the World

The students had experienced so much at the festival already, and each new experience had filled them with wonder. They had danced, listened to stories, tried on clothes, and learned new words. Now, as they gathered around Ms. Lopez, they noticed a delicious aroma drifting through the air. The scent was warm, spicy, and sweet all at once, making their mouths water and their stomachs rumble in anticipation. They knew that it was finally time for one of the festival activities they'd been most excited about—sampling food from around the world.

Ms. Lopez led them toward a lively food pavilion, where the air was thick with the aromas of cooking and the sound of laughter and chatter. The tent was lined with stalls, each one showcasing a different type of food, with colorful banners and menus written in a variety of languages. The students marveled at the variety; there were foods they recognized, like bread and rice dishes, and others they had never seen before, prepared in ways they couldn't have imagined. Some dishes steamed in large pots, while others were grilled, baked, or fried, each one adding its own unique fragrance to the mix.

A friendly man named Ravi welcomed the students with a smile as they entered the pavilion. He explained that each stall represented a different region or country, and that every dish had a story to tell. "Food is a way of sharing a piece of one's culture," he said, his voice warm and inviting. "Each flavor, each spice, tells a story about the people who make it, the places they come from, and the traditions they carry. Today, you'll get to taste those stories."

The students listened intently, intrigued by the idea that food could hold history and meaning. They hadn't thought much about where food came from beyond the kitchen, but as they looked around the pavilion, they began to understand that each dish was part of a larger story—a story about people, land, and tradition.

Ms. Lopez gave each student a small tasting plate and encouraged them to approach the stalls, to be curious and open-minded, and to try foods that might seem unfamiliar. She reminded them of the importance of being respectful, not only by trying each food with appreciation but also by understanding that for some people, these dishes were tied to memories, celebrations, and family gatherings.

The students dispersed, each one eager to explore. Mia found herself at a stall that offered small bites of grilled vegetables, spiced with flavors she didn't recognize. The vendor, an elderly woman with a kind smile, handed her a sample and explained that the vegetables were marinated in a special blend of spices, meant to bring out the flavors of the earth. Mia hesitated for a moment, unsure of the strong, smoky smell, but then took a small bite. The flavors burst on her tongue—earthy, spicy, and tangy all at once. It was unlike anything she had tasted before, and though she wasn't sure if she loved it, she appreciated the way the flavors felt bold and unique. She wrote in her notebook, "Food can be surprising," realizing that flavors could open her mind to new sensations.

Ethan, always ready for an adventure, headed straight for a stall where the vendor was serving a dish of rice topped with a thick, aromatic sauce. The vendor explained that this dish was a staple in her country, something families often shared around the dinner table. Ethan took a big bite, savoring the warmth and spice of the sauce. It was rich, with hints of cinnamon and cloves, and the rice was fluffy and comforting. He grinned, feeling like he was eating a piece of a family tradition. "It's like tasting home," he thought, imagining families around the world enjoying this dish together.

Jackson, who often stuck to familiar foods, found himself in front of a table filled with small, round pastries that looked like little pillows. The vendor explained that they were stuffed with a sweet, nutty filling made from ground nuts and honey. Jackson took a hesitant bite, and the sweetness of the honey mixed with the crunch of the nuts surprised him. It was richer and more complex than the desserts he was used to, and he felt a sense of awe at the intricate flavors. "It's like dessert, but with history," he thought, scribbling in his notebook.

Emma, drawn to fresh and colorful dishes, stopped at a stall where a woman was offering small, colorful salads. Each salad was topped with a dressing made from citrus and herbs, which gave it a bright, tangy flavor. Emma took a bite, feeling the crispness of the vegetables and the sharpness of the citrus blend on her tongue. The vendor explained that this salad was often eaten in warm climates, where the fresh ingredients helped keep people cool and refreshed. Emma felt a new appreciation for how food could reflect the land and climate, a connection between nature and nourishment.

Liam, who had always been fascinated by cooking, found himself captivated by a dish with a rich, savory aroma. The vendor was stirring a pot filled with a stew made from lentils, tomatoes, and a blend of spices that filled the air with warmth. Liam took a small bowl and tasted the stew, surprised by the depth of the flavors. It was hearty, comforting, and filled with spices he couldn't quite name. The vendor explained that this dish was often shared during family gatherings, a way of bringing people together around a meal. Liam felt inspired, realizing that food could be a way of showing care and connection.

As the students continued tasting, they began to understand that food was more than just nourishment—it was an expression of love, heritage, and community. Each dish had a story, each flavor a reason. They moved from stall to stall, tasting bites that ranged from sweet to savory, spicy to mild, and everything in between. Some foods surprised them with bold flavors they hadn't expected, while others comforted them with familiar tastes in unfamiliar forms.

Sophia, who loved sweets, was delighted to find a stall offering small pieces of a dessert made from coconut and sugar, shaped into delicate rounds and sprinkled with tiny seeds. The vendor explained that this dessert was often shared during festivals and celebrations, a treat that symbolized joy and togetherness. Sophia took a bite, savoring the sweetness and the light, chewy texture. It was simple yet delicious, and she could imagine sharing it with friends and family. "Food can be a celebration," she wrote, smiling as she imagined the festivals where people gathered to share this treat.

    By the time they had tasted food from nearly every stall, the students were full, their plates empty, but their minds overflowing with new ideas and flavors. They had tried things they'd never imagined, tasted ingredients they couldn't name, and learned about the importance of food in connecting people to their culture and each other.

Chapter 12: Traditions of Togetherness

After the vibrant experience of tasting foods from around the world, Ms. Lopez's class made their way toward a large, open space with rows of tables arranged under a colorful canopy of flags and banners. The tables were decorated with flowers, small artifacts, and beautifully crafted candles that flickered softly in the afternoon light. The area had an inviting, cozy atmosphere that seemed to draw everyone in, hinting at the idea of gathering, sharing, and togetherness. The students could feel something special about this place—a sense of community and warmth that went beyond words.

Ms. Lopez gathered the students around, explaining that this part of the festival was dedicated to learning about the many traditions of togetherness that people across the world celebrate. She described how each table represented a different custom, a tradition from a culture that cherished the idea of bringing people together. These traditions could be ceremonies, festivals, or simple everyday practices that bound families and friends closer. She encouraged her students to explore the tables, talk to the hosts, and learn about how people celebrate and connect.

Their guide for this part of the festival was a woman named Nadia, who wore a warm smile and a welcoming expression. She explained that traditions of togetherness were ways in which people created bonds and showed appreciation for one another. "These traditions remind us of what we share and what makes life special," she said. "They teach us that no matter where we are in the world, we all seek moments of connection, celebration, and gratitude with those we care about."

The students listened closely, intrigued by the idea of customs centered around togetherness. They hadn't thought much about how different cultures celebrate unity, love, and friendship in unique ways. As they looked around at the tables, each displaying something different, they felt a growing sense of curiosity and excitement. Ms.

Lopez encouraged them to choose tables that interested them and to ask questions, assuring them that the festival hosts would be happy to share the stories behind each tradition.

Mia was drawn to a table adorned with small candles and intricate, handwoven cloths. The host, an older woman with a gentle demeanor, introduced herself as Lila and explained that the table represented a tradition from her culture called "The Night of Lights." She described how families would gather on a certain night each year, lighting candles together as a way of showing gratitude for the light in their lives. Each candle represented a wish or a memory, and families would spend the evening sharing stories, singing songs, and enjoying each other's company.

Mia was fascinated by this tradition, especially the idea of lighting candles to honor memories and dreams. She could imagine families gathered together, their faces illuminated by the warm glow of candlelight, sharing stories and hopes. She felt moved by the simplicity and beauty of the ritual, understanding how it could bring people closer. She wrote in her notebook, "Togetherness can be as simple as lighting a candle," wanting to remember that togetherness didn't always require grand gestures but could be found in small, meaningful actions.

Ethan, always drawn to lively activities, was attracted to a table that displayed drums, colorful scarves, and festive decorations. The host explained that this table represented a dance celebration called "Unity Day," a tradition where entire communities gathered to dance and sing together. People wore bright clothes and joined hands, forming a large circle that symbolized unity and harmony. The festival was a way for people of all ages to come together, to move to the same rhythm, and to celebrate their connections.

Ethan listened eagerly, imagining the energy and joy of such a celebration. He loved the idea of dancing as a way to express togetherness, a way to bring people together in a circle where everyone could feel included. He jotted down in his notebook, "Togetherness can be loud and full of energy," understanding that celebration could be both joyful and deeply meaningful.

Emma found herself captivated by a table displaying delicate, handmade crafts. The host, a young woman named Suri, explained that in her culture, people celebrated togetherness through a tradition of gift-giving. On special occasions, families and friends would gather to exchange small, handmade gifts, each one crafted with love and thought. The gifts were often symbolic, representing wishes for health, happiness, or good fortune. Suri described how each gift was wrapped in fabric and presented with a few words of kindness or a simple blessing.

Emma felt touched by this tradition, realizing that even a small, thoughtful gift could carry a lot of meaning. She could imagine people sharing these gifts, watching each other's faces light up as they unwrapped something crafted just for them. She wrote in her notebook, "Togetherness is giving something from the heart," appreciating how these gifts were more than just objects; they were symbols of love and thoughtfulness.

Jackson, who was curious about traditions related to food, visited a table where a large pot of stew simmered over a small flame. The host, a man named Paulo, explained that this table represented a tradition called "Family Stew Night." Once a month, families and friends would gather to cook and share a big pot of stew, each person bringing an ingredient to contribute. As the stew cooked, everyone would share stories, laugh, and bond over the meal. The stew became a symbol of community, with each ingredient representing the contributions of everyone involved.

Jackson loved the idea of everyone bringing something to add to the meal, seeing how the stew was a metaphor for how each person's contribution mattered. He could picture families sitting around, smelling the delicious aroma, and sharing their lives with one another. He wrote down in his notebook, "Togetherness is everyone bringing something to the table," understanding that community was about each person's unique contribution.

Liam, who enjoyed quiet and reflective activities, was drawn to a table decorated with small stones and flowers. The host, an elderly man named Tarek, explained that this table represented a tradition called "The Garden of Remembrance." Families would gather each year in a quiet garden, where they would place stones inscribed with the names of loved ones or with words of gratitude. The garden was a peaceful place where people could reflect on their blessings and honor those who had passed on.

Liam found this tradition deeply moving, appreciating the quiet reverence of remembering loved ones in such a gentle, respectful way. He could imagine families gathered in the garden, each person laying a stone and sharing a memory or a word of gratitude. He wrote in his notebook, "Togetherness can be remembering those we love," seeing that togetherness could also be about honoring the past and cherishing memories.

Sophia, drawn to vibrant decorations, stopped at a table with an array of painted eggs and colorful flowers. The host explained that this tradition, called "Festival of New Beginnings," celebrated the arrival of spring and new life. Families would gather to paint eggs, each one representing a wish or a hope for the coming year. The painted eggs were then displayed in a basket, symbolizing the collective hopes of the family and community.

Sophia loved the idea of celebrating new beginnings and wishes, especially through something as simple as painting an egg. She could picture families gathering, each person adding their own wish to the basket, creating a collection of hopes and dreams. She jotted down in her notebook, "Togetherness is celebrating new beginnings," inspired by the way people could come together to look toward the future with hope.

As the students continued exploring, they found that each table offered a different perspective on what it meant to be together, to share, and to celebrate life. Each tradition was unique, yet they all carried a common thread—the importance of coming together to create moments of connection, gratitude, and joy. They began to see that while cultures might differ in how they expressed these values, the desire to connect, to remember, and to celebrate was universal.

Chapter 13: Lessons in Craftsmanship

As the festival day continued, Ms. Lopez gathered her students to move on to the next activity. They had already explored so much—the foods, stories, and dances of cultures from around the world—but now they were about to enter a tent that showcased something different: the art of craftsmanship. This part of the festival was dedicated to showing how people from various cultures used their hands, tools, and creativity to make items that were not just useful but also beautiful and meaningful. The air was filled with a sense of anticipation as the students entered, eager to see what wonders awaited them inside.

The tent was filled with tables and booths where artisans demonstrated skills they had learned and honed over years, sometimes passed down through generations. Each workstation was dedicated to a different craft: pottery, weaving, basket-making, carving, and metalworking. The students moved slowly, their eyes wide as they took in the sights. They could see artisans carefully shaping clay on a pottery wheel, weaving intricate patterns with colorful threads, or carving delicate designs into wood. The tent felt alive with focus and creativity, a place where each piece of work told a story of patience, tradition, and skill.

Their guide for this section of the festival was a woman named Amara, who welcomed them with a warm smile. She wore a handwoven shawl decorated with small embroidered patterns, each one symbolizing a different aspect of nature—a leaf, a wave, a mountain. Amara explained that the crafts they would see today were part of people's everyday lives in many parts of the world. They weren't just hobbies; they were skills that had been essential for survival and for expressing identity. "These crafts are ways people connect to their heritage," she said. "Every piece has a purpose, and every craftsperson has a story to tell through their hands."

The students were quiet, listening intently. Amara's words helped them realize that craftsmanship wasn't just about creating something beautiful; it was about understanding the journey, the skill, and the story behind each piece. Ms. Lopez encouraged them to ask questions, to observe closely, and to appreciate the dedication and focus of the artisans they were about to meet.

Mia was immediately drawn to the pottery table, where an older woman sat in front of a spinning pottery wheel, her hands shaping a lump of clay with careful, practiced movements. The woman introduced herself as Rosa and explained that she had learned pottery from her grandmother, who had learned it from her mother before her. She showed Mia how she used her fingers to guide the clay, feeling its texture and shaping it into a pot. As Mia watched, she noticed how focused Rosa was, her hands moving smoothly and purposefully, shaping the clay with a gentle strength.

Rosa handed Mia a small lump of clay and invited her to try shaping it herself. Mia pressed her fingers into the clay, feeling its coolness and pliability. She tried to copy Rosa's movements, but the clay didn't quite cooperate, and her pot quickly turned into a lopsided bowl. Rosa chuckled kindly, guiding Mia's hands and showing her how to keep the clay balanced on the wheel. "It takes patience and practice," she said gently. "Every potter has made lopsided pots at first. Each mistake teaches you something new."

Mia felt a sense of admiration for Rosa, realizing how much patience and skill went into each piece of pottery. She could see that crafting pottery wasn't just about making something useful; it was about learning, growing, and connecting with tradition. She scribbled in her notebook, "Patience makes beautiful things," wanting to remember this lesson.

Nearby, Ethan was watching a basket weaver at work, fascinated by the way the artisan wove long strips of straw together to form the shape of a basket. The weaver, a man named Babu, explained that basket-making was a skill passed down in his family for generations. Each basket he made was unique, but they all followed a basic structure that had been used for centuries. As Babu wove, he explained how the baskets were used for carrying food, storing items, and even for ceremonies.

Ethan was struck by the idea that something as simple as a basket could be so versatile, so essential to daily life. Babu invited Ethan to try weaving a few strands himself, guiding his hands as he looped the straw over and under, creating a small section of the basket's pattern. Ethan's fingers fumbled at first, but soon he found a rhythm, enjoying the repetitive, calming nature of the task. He realized that basket-weaving wasn't just a skill; it was a way of bringing order and beauty to something as ordinary as carrying food or storing belongings. In his notebook, he wrote, "Crafting is finding beauty in the everyday."

Emma was drawn to a station where a young woman named Zara was weaving a piece of fabric on a loom. The loom was large, with dozens of colorful threads stretched across it, creating a beautiful, intricate design as Zara wove each row carefully. Emma watched, mesmerized by the colors and patterns, and asked Zara about the meaning behind them. Zara explained that the colors and patterns she used had significance; they represented different elements of her culture and were used to tell stories about family, nature, and community.

Emma was fascinated by the idea that a simple piece of cloth could carry so much meaning. Zara showed her how to add a few rows to the weaving, guiding her hands gently as Emma lifted and lowered the threads. The process was rhythmic, almost meditative, and Emma could see how weaving could be both an art and a form of storytelling. She wrote in her notebook, "Weaving is telling a story without words," inspired by the way each row added to the tapestry's beauty and meaning.

Jackson found himself at a table where an older man named Kai was carving a piece of wood. Kai's hands were strong and steady as he carefully carved out a delicate design, transforming the wood into a small, intricate sculpture. Jackson was amazed at the level of detail Kai achieved, wondering how he could create something so delicate from such a solid material. Kai explained that carving required both strength and gentleness, knowing when to push hard and when to be soft. Each piece he carved held a different meaning, whether it was an animal, a symbol, or a simple pattern.

Kai handed Jackson a small block of wood and a carving tool, guiding him through a simple pattern. Jackson's hands felt clumsy, but with Kai's guidance, he managed to carve a few lines into the wood. He was amazed at how difficult it was, realizing how much control and patience carving required. He wrote in his notebook, "Carving is learning to be strong and gentle," appreciating how craftsmanship could teach balance and control.

Liam, who loved anything related to tools and construction, was drawn to a table where a metalworker named Anya was shaping a small piece of copper into a delicate bracelet. She explained that metalworking was both an art and a science, requiring an understanding of the material's properties as well as skill with tools. Anya showed Liam how to use a small hammer to shape the metal, explaining that each tap had to be precise, balancing strength with care.

Liam tried shaping a piece of metal, guided by Anya's steady hand. He was amazed by how the copper softened and took shape under the hammer's force, transforming from a flat piece into something beautiful. He realized that metalworking was not only about creating something useful but also about respecting the material, understanding its strengths and limitations. He wrote in his notebook, "Craftsmanship is respecting the material," realizing that true skill involved understanding both one's tools and the materials they worked with.

Sophia was drawn to a table where a woman named Leila was creating jewelry with small beads and stones. Each bead was threaded carefully onto a thin string, creating intricate patterns and designs. Leila explained that each piece of jewelry was made with intention, designed to represent something important. In her culture, certain colors and stones held specific meanings, like love, protection, or courage.

Chapter 14: The World of Folktales and Legends

After leaving the craftsmanship tent, Ms. Lopez's class continued their journey through the festival grounds, their minds filled with thoughts about the artistry they had just witnessed. Each student carried with them a sense of respect for the dedication and love that went into every handmade item, and they felt enriched by the experience. But as they moved further, they found themselves drawn to a quieter corner of the festival, where soft music and gentle laughter filled the air. In this corner, the atmosphere was calm and inviting, with cushioned seating arranged around a small platform decorated with rugs, lanterns, and tapestries. A large sign above the area read: "The World of Folktales and Legends."

Ms. Lopez gathered the students in a semicircle, and they quickly realized that this space was designed for storytelling. They had already heard stories throughout the festival, but they could tell that this would be something different. The scene felt magical, like stepping into another world. The lanterns cast a soft glow, and the colorful rugs looked as if they'd been collected from all over the world. The students settled down quietly, sensing that they were about to experience something truly special.

Their storyteller for this part of the day was a man named Ravi, who wore a loose, colorful robe and had a long, gray beard that made him look as though he'd stepped right out of a story himself. His eyes sparkled as he looked at the group, and he welcomed them with a deep, warm voice. Ravi explained that folktales and legends were more than just stories; they were pieces of history, windows into cultures, and lessons passed down through generations. "Each tale holds a truth, a lesson, or a glimpse into the beliefs of the people who tell it," he said.

"These stories are part of who we are, connecting us to the past and guiding us into the future."

The students listened intently, drawn in by Ravi's words. He explained that folktales could include magical creatures, wise animals, or brave heroes, and that every character, no matter how fantastical, carried a piece of wisdom that was meant to be shared. He asked the students to let their imaginations run free, to picture the places and people he would describe, and to find meaning in each tale.

Ravi began with a story called "The Tale of the Silver Moon." He described a village nestled deep in the mountains, where the people depended on the moonlight to guide them home each night. But one night, the moon disappeared, leaving the village shrouded in darkness. The villagers were frightened and worried, but a young girl named Lina volunteered to journey to the top of the tallest mountain to find the moon and bring it back.

As Ravi spoke, his voice became softer and more intense, painting a picture of Lina's bravery. The students could imagine her climbing the steep, rocky slopes, determined to help her village. Ravi described how Lina found the moon trapped behind a cloud, and with her kind words and gentle heart, she convinced the cloud to release it. The moon returned to the sky, and the villagers celebrated Lina's courage and kindness.

The students were mesmerized, their eyes wide with wonder. They could feel the story's magic, and they understood the lesson beneath it—that courage could come from a place of kindness and that helping others was a powerful form of bravery. Mia wrote in her notebook, "Bravery doesn't need strength; it needs heart," wanting to remember Lina's gentle courage.

Ravi continued with another story, "The Clever Fox and the Hungry Wolf." In this tale, a fox and a wolf lived near a forest filled with delicious berries, but the wolf, too greedy to share, always chased the fox away. One day, the fox, clever and quick-thinking, tricked the wolf by leading him into a trap of brambles. The wolf struggled and failed to escape, while the fox happily collected berries to share with other animals who had helped him.

The students laughed at the fox's cleverness and admired his generosity. Ravi explained that many folktales used animals as symbols, representing qualities like cleverness, greed, kindness, or bravery. Jackson was especially taken with the fox, writing down, "Sometimes the smartest are the ones who share," realizing that the fox's cleverness lay not just in tricking the wolf but in being kind to others.

The next story, "The Rainbow Bridge," was about two villages separated by a wide river. The people of each village often argued and rarely spoke to one another. But one day, a terrible storm washed away the bridge that connected them. When the sky cleared, a young boy from one village and a girl from the other decided to build a new bridge together, despite the old feuds. As they worked, a rainbow appeared in the sky, symbolizing the bridge of peace they were creating. When the villagers saw this, they joined in, and the two villages became friends once more.

This story left the students quiet, each of them moved by the image of the rainbow bridge. Ravi explained that some legends were told to inspire unity and kindness, to remind people that even old arguments could be overcome with a little understanding. Emma wrote in her notebook, "Peace is a bridge we build together," feeling the importance of connection and kindness in her heart.

Ravi went on to tell several more tales, each one filled with meaning and mystery. There was the story of the "Golden Fish," a magical creature that granted wishes to a humble fisherman who showed it kindness, and "The Singing Tree," a tree that grew in the heart of a desert and only sang for those who were truly patient and listened with open hearts. Each tale was different, yet they all spoke to values like kindness, patience, humility, and courage.

THE BIG FIELD TRIP

As Ravi told his stories, he would often pause to ask the students what they thought certain symbols meant or why they thought a character acted in a certain way. The students responded thoughtfully, offering ideas about what bravery looked like, why kindness was powerful, or how forgiveness could heal old wounds. Ravi listened to each answer, nodding thoughtfully, and encouraging them to look deeper into the meanings hidden within the tales.

One of the final stories Ravi shared was called "The Stone of Generosity." It was about a traveler who came to a village with nothing but a small, smooth stone. The villagers, curious and a bit suspicious, asked him what he planned to do with it. The traveler explained that he would make a soup using the stone as a magical ingredient, but he needed a few other items to bring out its flavor. One by one, the villagers brought him vegetables, spices, and even a few pieces of meat to add to the pot. In the end, the traveler created a delicious soup, which everyone shared together. The villagers realized that the true magic of the stone was that it brought them together, each person contributing something to create something bigger than themselves.

Ethan laughed at the cleverness of the traveler but understood the deeper message of the story. He realized that the traveler's stone had taught the villagers the power of giving and sharing, how small contributions could make a big difference. He wrote in his notebook, "Giving makes everything richer," feeling a new appreciation for generosity and cooperation.

Ravi finished his storytelling session with a short poem about the stars, explaining that in his culture, the stars represented the wisdom of ancestors watching over and guiding them. He reminded the students that folktales and legends were gifts from those who came before, passed down to keep traditions, lessons, and memories alive.

Ms. Lopez invited the students to reflect on the stories they had heard and to share their favorite parts. One by one, the students spoke about the stories that resonated with them, the characters they admired, and the lessons they wanted to carry forward. Mia shared her admiration for Lina's gentle bravery, while Jackson talked about the clever fox's generosity. Emma reflected on the rainbow bridge story, saying that it had made her realize the importance of friendship and understanding.

As each student spoke, Ravi listened closely, nodding with approval at their insights. He encouraged them to remember that stories were meant to be shared, to inspire others, and to remind people of the values that connected them. He explained that each story held a piece of the culture it came from, a reminder of what was cherished and respected.

Chapter 15: Symbols of Identity and Belonging

After immersing themselves in the enchanting world of folktales and legends, Ms. Lopez led her class toward an exhibit that looked quieter but no less captivating. They approached a section of the festival dedicated to symbols of identity and belonging. This area was lined with display cases and tables, each one presenting items of significance from various cultures: amulets, charms, family crests, painted symbols, and objects adorned with meaningful colors and shapes. The students noticed the intricate carvings, the bold patterns, and the rich textures of the items before them, feeling the weight of history and identity in each piece.

Ms. Lopez gathered her students in a semicircle and introduced this part of their journey. She explained that the symbols and items they were about to see represented identity and belonging in different cultures. These symbols were not just decorations or artwork; they were chosen or created to tell stories about who people were, where they came from, and what they valued. "Symbols can mean different things to different people," she said. "They can represent families, communities, dreams, or even promises. Each one is a piece of history and a statement of identity."

As the students looked around, they began to understand that these objects weren't just artifacts—they were ways of expressing belonging, purpose, and pride. They realized that each item held a story or a memory, something important enough to pass down through generations. Ms. Lopez encouraged them to take their time, observe closely, and ask questions to learn about the stories behind each symbol.

Their guide for this exhibit was a woman named Sana, who wore a beautifully embroidered shawl adorned with small symbols that represented her family and heritage. She explained that each display in the exhibit represented different symbols of identity, each one carefully selected to show the diverse ways people express who they are and where they come from. "Some of these symbols are worn, some are kept in the home, and others are carried as reminders," she said. "But they all tell a story of connection—to family, to community, and to something larger than oneself."

The first table they approached held a collection of small, intricately carved animals, each one representing a different quality. Sana explained that in many cultures, animals were seen as symbols, each one carrying certain traits that people admired or aspired to embody. There was a small figure of an eagle, symbolizing strength and vision, a bear for courage, and a turtle for wisdom and patience. These animal symbols were often carried as charms, worn as jewelry, or even tattooed as reminders of the qualities they represented.

Jackson was immediately drawn to the eagle figure, fascinated by the idea of an animal representing strength and vision. He asked Sana why the eagle was chosen to represent these qualities, and she explained that eagles soar high above, seeing the world from a unique perspective. In many cultures, the eagle is a symbol of freedom and wisdom, inspiring people to see beyond their current view and to approach life with clarity. Jackson thought about this, realizing that the symbol wasn't just about the animal itself but what it stood for. He scribbled in his notebook, "Symbols can show us who we want to be," understanding that symbols could inspire people to strive for certain values.

At the next table, Emma found herself captivated by a set of colorful woven belts, each one adorned with intricate patterns. Sana explained that in some cultures, these belts were worn as a way to express family heritage or tribal affiliation. The patterns were unique to each family or community, representing generations of tradition and pride. By wearing these belts, people carried their heritage with them, a symbol of belonging that could be seen by others.

Emma asked if the patterns had specific meanings, and Sana nodded, explaining that each shape and color represented something important—maybe a mountain, a river, or even a family motto. The belts were not just decorative; they were personal statements of identity, linking people to their ancestors and their land. Emma thought about this, feeling a newfound respect for something as simple as a belt, realizing it could carry so much significance. In her notebook, she wrote, "Clothes can hold history," inspired by the idea that identity could be woven into something worn every day.

Ethan's attention was captured by a display of shields painted with bold designs. Sana explained that these shields were used in ceremonies and battles, symbols of protection, strength, and community. Each design represented a specific group, and by carrying or displaying the shield, people showed their allegiance and pride in their heritage. The shields were not just weapons; they were symbols of honor and unity, a way for people to stand together and show their strength as a group.

Ethan found this fascinating, especially the idea of a shield as a symbol beyond its function. He realized that people could feel stronger and more connected by carrying symbols that represented their community. It wasn't just about physical protection; it was about emotional and spiritual strength, about belonging to something greater. He wrote in his notebook, "Symbols make us feel part of something," understanding that identity wasn't just individual—it was collective.

Sophia was drawn to a collection of amulets and talismans, each one unique in shape and material. Some were made of metal, others of stone or wood, and each had a distinct design. Sana explained that these amulets were carried as symbols of protection or luck, each one chosen carefully for its meaning. Some people carried them for courage, others for health or prosperity, and many were passed down through families, becoming cherished heirlooms.

Sophia asked about a small, heart-shaped amulet made of polished stone, and Sana explained that it was a symbol of love and protection, often given to children by their parents. This small object held the hopes and wishes of a family, a way of carrying love and safety wherever the child went. Sophia thought about how an object could hold so much feeling, realizing that symbols didn't always have to be visible or public; sometimes, they were quiet, personal reminders of love and care. In her notebook, she wrote, "Symbols are like a hug you carry with you."

Liam was intrigued by a display of rings and necklaces adorned with family crests and intricate engravings. Sana explained that these pieces were often worn to represent a family's history or values. Each crest or design told a story, a symbol that represented generations of family members. The students looked closely at the designs, noticing lions, trees, and crowns among the patterns, each one signifying strength, growth, or leadership.

Liam asked Sana if every family had a crest, and she explained that while not every family did, many cultures had ways of symbolizing family pride and unity. The crests were like a shared identity, something that connected people to their ancestors and to each other. Liam wrote in his notebook, "Family symbols show where we come from," realizing that identity could be both personal and shared, a bridge between the past and the future.

Mia was captivated by a section of painted rocks, each one decorated with vibrant colors and patterns. Sana explained that these rocks were symbols of friendship and community, exchanged among friends or given as gifts to welcome someone into a group. Each rock was unique, representing the individuality of the giver and the bond of the relationship. By painting and sharing these rocks, people showed their commitment to friendship and kindness.

Mia picked up a rock with a simple, heart-shaped design and thought about the friends in her life. She loved the idea that symbols could be used to strengthen bonds and show people they were valued. In her notebook, she wrote, "Symbols can be small but mean a lot," understanding that even simple acts could hold deep meaning.

The students continued exploring, moving from display to display and taking in the stories behind each symbol. They saw how symbols of identity could be worn, carried, or shared, and how each one reflected the beliefs, values, and connections that people held dear. They realized that identity wasn't just something internal; it was something people expressed and celebrated with symbols, colors, and objects that connected them to their culture, family, and community.

Chapter 16: Music of the World

With a new appreciation for symbols of identity and the ways people around the world express who they are, Ms. Lopez's class continued on their journey. The students walked eagerly, their minds buzzing with thoughts of amulets, crests, and painted rocks. They were almost surprised to find themselves standing in front of another tent, smaller and cozier than some of the others but vibrant with sound. The tent was alive with melodies, rhythms, and the hum of voices, blending together in a way that made each student want to stop, listen, and explore. This was the Music of the World tent, and it welcomed them with sounds from every corner of the globe.

Ms. Lopez led her class inside, where they were greeted by a man named Luis, who wore a wide smile and an enthusiasm that matched the lively energy of the music. Luis introduced himself as both a musician and a music teacher, explaining that he had dedicated his life to learning and sharing music from different cultures. "Music is a language everyone can understand," he told the students warmly. "It doesn't matter where you come from or what language you speak—music is a way for people to connect, to share joy, and to tell stories."

As the students looked around, they noticed that the tent was filled with instruments of all shapes and sizes. There were drums, flutes, stringed instruments, and even a few unusual pieces that looked like they had been handcrafted from materials found in nature. Each instrument seemed to carry its own personality, its own sound waiting to be released. Some looked ancient and weathered, while others were brightly painted and beautifully polished. Luis explained that each instrument held a piece of the culture it came from, a way for people to express themselves and to pass down their traditions through music.

The first instrument Luis introduced was a large, drum-like instrument called a djembe. He explained that it was originally from

West Africa and was often used in gatherings where people would play and dance together. The djembe was powerful, its deep sound resonating in the students' chests as Luis struck it with his hands. He invited them to gather in a circle, explaining that drums were often used to create a communal rhythm, a heartbeat that connected everyone who listened or danced along.

Jackson was one of the first to reach out, eager to feel the rhythm of the djembe. Luis showed him how to strike the drum, creating different sounds by hitting it in different spots. Jackson tried his best to mimic Luis's movements, grinning as he heard the drum respond to his touch. As he played, he felt a connection to the rhythm, a feeling that the beat was something shared and ancient. Jackson wrote in his notebook, "Music is a heartbeat we share," realizing that rhythm was something everyone could feel, no matter where they were from.

Next, Luis picked up a flute made from bamboo, explaining that it was commonly used in the mountains of South America. He demonstrated how to play, creating soft, haunting notes that seemed to float through the air like whispers. The students listened, captivated by the sound, which felt peaceful yet powerful, as though it carried secrets of nature and mountains. Luis explained that in some cultures, the flute was used to imitate the sounds of birds, streams, and winds, allowing people to feel connected to the natural world.

Emma was intrigued by the flute's gentle sound and asked if she could try it. Luis handed it to her carefully, guiding her fingers to the right spots and showing her how to blow softly. Emma struggled at first, but after a few tries, she managed to create a soft, breathy note. She felt a sense of wonder at the flute's simplicity and beauty, realizing that even something as small as a bamboo stick could create something magical. She wrote in her notebook, "Music lets us speak with nature," inspired by the way the flute's sound seemed to echo the world outside.

The students moved on to another corner of the tent, where Luis introduced them to a stringed instrument called the kora. He explained that the kora came from West Africa and was often used to tell stories and share history. The instrument looked almost like a cross between a guitar and a harp, with a round body and long strings stretching upward. Luis plucked the strings carefully, creating a melody that was both gentle and vibrant, like a conversation between the notes. He told them that kora players, called griots, were often seen as storytellers and historians, preserving the memories of their communities through music.

Mia was fascinated by the kora's sound and asked if she could try plucking a few strings. Luis showed her how to hold the instrument and place her fingers, guiding her as she plucked each string gently. She felt the vibration of each note under her fingertips, as if the music were alive and speaking to her. Mia wrote in her notebook, "Music can hold memories," understanding that the kora was more than just an instrument; it was a keeper of stories and history.

As they continued exploring, Luis led them to an area where a collection of bells and small percussion instruments were displayed. He explained that in some cultures, bells were used in ceremonies to create rhythms and invite people to gather. Each bell had its own unique sound, and Luis demonstrated how they could be played together to create layers of rhythm and melody. He explained that bells were often seen as symbols of joy and celebration, used to mark special occasions and to invite people to join in music-making.

Ethan, always ready for something lively, picked up a small bell and shook it with enthusiasm. The bright, clear sound filled the air, making everyone smile. Luis encouraged the other students to join in, handing out bells, rattles, and small drums so they could create their own rhythm together. The students laughed as they found their beat, each one adding their own sound to the mix. Ethan wrote in his notebook, "Music is for everyone," realizing that playing music didn't have to be complicated or perfect—it was about sharing joy and creating something together.

Luis then introduced them to an instrument called the sitar, a stringed instrument from South Asia. Its long neck and intricately decorated body made it look almost like a work of art. Luis explained that the sitar was often used to play meditative and complex melodies, each note flowing into the next with precision and emotion. He plucked the strings gently, creating a melody that was both calming and deep, filling the tent with a sense of peace.

Sophia asked if she could try the sitar, and Luis showed her how to hold it and gently pluck the strings. She was amazed by the complexity of the sounds, each note resonating with a richness she hadn't expected. She realized that some music was meant to be listened to deeply, to be felt in a way that went beyond words. She wrote in her notebook, "Music can bring us peace," understanding that sound could soothe and connect people to a sense of inner calm.

Luis continued to introduce more instruments, each one unique and filled with history. There was the didgeridoo from Australia, a long, hollow instrument that created a deep, droning sound, often used to tell stories of the land and its people. There were hand drums from different cultures, each one carrying a unique rhythm and purpose, some used in spiritual ceremonies and others in celebrations. Each instrument carried its own story, a way for people to express themselves and connect with each other.

The students were amazed by the diversity of sounds, realizing that music was more than just entertainment—it was a way of preserving culture, expressing identity, and bringing people together. As they moved through the tent, they tried each instrument with a sense of wonder and respect, realizing that every sound carried meaning and that every instrument was a language of its own.

Chapter 17: The Power of Words and Poetry

The next stop on Ms. Lopez's class journey through the multicultural festival took them to a tent that felt quieter, yet somehow filled with an intangible energy. As they approached, they noticed that the tent was decorated with strings of paper lanterns and colorful banners, each displaying quotes and phrases in different languages. Words like "peace," "hope," and "dream" floated through the air, written in scripts that were both familiar and foreign to the students. The tent was dedicated to the Power of Words and Poetry, a space that celebrated the magic of language in all its forms.

Ms. Lopez led her students into the tent, where a gentle man named Amir greeted them. His voice was soft yet rich, and he spoke with a cadence that made his words feel like music. Amir welcomed them with a poem, reciting it slowly in a language the students didn't understand. Yet even though they didn't know the meaning of the words, the rhythm and flow of his voice filled them with a sense of calm and curiosity. After he finished, Amir smiled and explained that poetry was like music for the soul, a way for people to express what they felt deeply.

He explained that today they would explore the power of words, learning how different cultures used language and poetry to express emotions, celebrate life, and connect with others. He told them that words, just like art and music, had the ability to bring people together. "Poetry is a gift," he said, "and it's something that belongs to everyone. When we share words, we share pieces of ourselves, our dreams, and our hopes."

The students settled down on soft cushions scattered around the tent, each one intrigued by the thought that words could hold such power. Ms. Lopez encouraged them to open their minds and hearts, to listen carefully, and to consider how words could shape their thoughts and feelings.

Amir began by explaining that poetry and storytelling were among the oldest forms of expression, used by people around the world to pass down history, values, and beliefs. He shared that in many cultures, poetry was spoken aloud, woven into everyday life and ceremonies, and celebrated as a way to connect with others. Each poem, he told them, was like a small window into someone's soul, a glimpse into what they felt, dreamed, or wished for.

He started with a poem from his own culture, one that had been passed down for generations. The poem spoke of hope and resilience, describing a river that flowed endlessly through difficult terrain, never stopping or giving up. As Amir recited the poem, his voice grew soft, like the whisper of a stream, then strong, like the surge of rapids. The students listened, captivated by the sound and rhythm, feeling as though they were on a journey with the river.

Mia was particularly moved by the poem, sensing its power even though she didn't know every word. She felt a deep connection to the river's journey, its resilience, and its strength. She wrote in her notebook, "Words can carry us," realizing that poetry had the power to transport her to places she'd never been, to make her feel emotions that were both hers and beyond her own experience.

Amir then recited another poem, this one from a distant land, filled with imagery of stars, the night sky, and the vastness of the universe. The poem was about wonder and curiosity, describing how the stars had guided travelers and dreamers throughout history, lighting up their paths and filling their hearts with hope. The words painted a picture of a world that was both mysterious and comforting, as though the stars were guardians watching over all.

Emma was fascinated by the poem, drawn to the images of stars and night. She felt a sense of awe as she listened, realizing that the same stars in the poem shone over her and everyone else around the world.

The poem made her feel connected to something bigger, something timeless. She wrote in her notebook, "Words can connect us to the universe," feeling as though she had glimpsed something vast and beautiful through the poet's words.

Next, Amir introduced the students to a form of poetry called haiku, a type of short Japanese poem that captured a moment in just a few lines. He explained that haikus were often inspired by nature, focusing on simple yet powerful images that captured a feeling or an observation. He recited a few haikus, each one describing a different season—spring blossoms, summer rain, autumn leaves, and winter snow. The poems were so brief, yet each one painted a vivid picture in the students' minds.

Sophia loved the haikus, appreciating their simplicity and beauty. She was amazed at how much emotion could be expressed in just a few words. She thought about how the haikus used simple images to convey deep feelings, realizing that poetry didn't have to be complicated to be powerful. She wrote in her notebook, "Words can be small but strong," inspired by the way the haikus captured so much in so little.

As the students continued to listen, Amir explained that many cultures used poetry to celebrate love, friendship, and kindness. He recited a poem from a Mediterranean country about friendship, describing it as a tree with roots that grew deep and strong, its branches providing shelter and shade. The words were warm and gentle, a tribute to the bonds that held people together. The students could almost feel the comfort and strength of the tree, a symbol of friendship that was lasting and supportive.

Jackson found himself drawn to the poem's message, thinking about his own friendships and how important they were to him. He felt a sense of gratitude for the friends he had, realizing that they were like the branches of the tree, providing strength and companionship. He wrote in his notebook, "Words remind us of who matters," understanding that poetry could be a way to celebrate the people he cared about.

Ethan was captivated by a poem about courage and dreams. The poem described a young bird standing at the edge of a cliff, unsure but determined to take flight. The words were filled with imagery of open skies, strong winds, and endless possibilities, conveying a message of bravery and hope. Ethan felt his heart lift as he listened, feeling the excitement and fear of the bird as if they were his own. He wrote in his notebook, "Words can give us courage," inspired by the way the poem encouraged him to pursue his own dreams.

Amir continued, introducing the students to poems about life's struggles and the strength to overcome them. He shared a poem about a mountain climber, a person who faced difficulties but never gave up, who reached the top and looked out over the world with pride and gratitude. The words were powerful, each line expressing resilience, determination, and the importance of never giving up. The students listened quietly, each one feeling the weight and strength of the climber's journey.

Chapter 18: Art of the Everyday

After the powerful experience with words and poetry, Ms. Lopez's class found themselves approaching another section of the festival. This area was filled with stalls, each one displaying ordinary items transformed by skill, creativity, and care. As they walked through the open-air market, the students noticed everyday objects like cups, plates, baskets, tools, and clothing, each one crafted with detail and beauty. This was the Art of the Everyday exhibit, a celebration of how simple items could be elevated into art when made with intention and love.

Ms. Lopez explained to the students that this part of the festival was about discovering the beauty in everyday life, showing them how items that were part of daily routines could also be expressions of creativity and culture. She told them to think about how each object was not just a tool or a piece of decoration, but something crafted by hand, often with unique designs or meaningful patterns. "These items," she said, "are more than just things to use—they're ways of expressing identity, tradition, and connection."

Their guide for this exhibit was a woman named Hana, whose friendly demeanor and gentle smile made the students feel welcome. Hana explained that each object in the market had been created by artisans who used their skills to make something both useful and beautiful. She encouraged the students to think about how art could be a part of everyday life, reminding them that creativity wasn't just for paintings or sculptures. "Every item here tells a story," Hana said. "Some tell of family, some of nature, and some of community. Every item was made with hands and heart, meant to bring beauty into people's daily routines."

The first stall they visited was filled with pottery, showcasing plates, cups, and bowls decorated with bright colors and intricate patterns. The students were fascinated by the swirls and shapes painted on each piece, some with floral designs, others with geometric patterns or animal motifs. Hana explained that in many cultures, pottery wasn't just a way to make eating or drinking more enjoyable—it was also a way to share stories and heritage. The patterns and colors often represented something important, like a family symbol or a connection to nature.

Mia was drawn to a deep blue bowl decorated with tiny white dots that looked like stars scattered across a night sky. She imagined someone eating from that bowl every day, perhaps thinking about the universe, the sky, or dreams. She held the bowl carefully, feeling its weight and admiring the smooth glaze. "It's amazing how something so simple can feel magical," she said quietly, realizing that even an everyday item could bring a little wonder into someone's life. She wrote in her notebook, "Everyday items can carry beauty and meaning," feeling a new appreciation for objects she might have once overlooked.

At the next stall, they found woven baskets of all shapes and sizes, each one beautifully crafted with patterns made from different shades of natural fibers. Hana explained that basket weaving was a tradition in many cultures, often passed down through generations. Each pattern represented something unique, whether it was a symbol of family, a tribute to nature, or simply a design that brought joy. She told the students that baskets were used for carrying food, storing tools, or even for ceremonies, making them both practical and beautiful.

Ethan picked up a small basket and examined the weave, impressed by the complexity of the pattern. He asked Hana how long it took to make a basket, and she explained that it could take hours or even days, depending on the size and design. Ethan was amazed by the dedication it took to create something so intricate, realizing that the basket was more than just a container—it was a work of art. He wrote in his notebook, "Crafting takes time, patience, and love," appreciating the skill and care that went into each piece.

Moving along, the students came to a stall displaying carved wooden spoons and utensils. Each spoon was unique, some with long, slender handles, others with wide bowls or delicate carvings. Hana explained that in some cultures, wooden utensils were carved with special patterns that held personal or family meaning. She shared that carving utensils was a skill that often required years to master, a way for artisans to bring beauty to the simplest tasks, like eating or cooking.

Jackson held a carved spoon, running his fingers over the delicate patterns etched into the handle. He was struck by the idea that something as ordinary as a spoon could be crafted with such care, as though it held a special purpose beyond eating. "It makes you want to be careful with it, to appreciate it," he said thoughtfully. He wrote in his notebook, "Ordinary things can be extraordinary," realizing that beauty could be found in even the smallest items.

At a nearby stall, they found colorful textiles—scarves, tablecloths, and blankets—each one handwoven and decorated with vibrant patterns. Hana explained that textiles were an essential part of daily life in many cultures, used for warmth, decoration, and even storytelling. The patterns and colors chosen often reflected local traditions, and each piece was crafted with intention, meant to last and be passed down through generations.

Sophia was fascinated by a blanket woven in shades of red, orange, and yellow, with symbols that resembled flames. Hana explained that the colors represented the sun and fire, symbols of warmth, energy, and life. Sophia thought about how a simple blanket could be so much more than just something to keep warm—it could be a reminder of the elements, of life's energy. She wrote in her notebook, "Everyday art connects us to nature," feeling a sense of wonder at how ordinary items could carry meaning.

The students continued exploring, visiting stalls with jewelry, decorated bowls, hand-painted mugs, and delicate fans. Each item seemed to hold a piece of its maker's heart, a bit of creativity infused into something people used every day. They realized that art wasn't limited to galleries or museums; it could be found in homes, markets, and even in the objects people used to carry food, decorate tables, or keep warm.

Liam was particularly drawn to a display of handmade fans, each one painted with scenes of mountains, rivers, or gardens. Hana explained that in some cultures, fans were more than just practical items—they were also symbols of grace and beauty, often given as gifts or used in celebrations. The students were amazed to learn that fans could carry messages or symbols, even serving as canvases for art and storytelling.

Liam held a fan decorated with a scene of a mountain under a full moon. He imagined someone using the fan on a warm summer night, feeling the cool air and admiring the painting. "It's like carrying a piece of nature with you," he said, realizing that art didn't have to be something big or complicated. He wrote in his notebook, "Everyday items can be works of art," appreciating the creativity that went into each fan.

Chapter 19: Games, Sports, and Team Spirit

The students could hardly contain their excitement as they approached the next area of the festival dedicated to games, sports, and team spirit. After exploring the beauty of everyday objects, the simplicity of crafted art, and the power of words and poetry, they were eager to experience a part of the festival that celebrated physical skill, playfulness, and unity. This area was set up like an outdoor playground and stadium combined, with colorful flags and banners displaying symbols from various games and sports played around the world.

Ms. Lopez gathered her students together and explained that the games and sports they would encounter here were more than just ways to exercise—they were reflections of culture, teamwork, and community values. "People from different parts of the world have created games that celebrate their skills, their beliefs, and their desire for friendly competition. Each game tells a story of cooperation, resilience, and joy," she said. She encouraged the students to keep an open mind, try new things, and, most importantly, enjoy the spirit of friendly play and teamwork.

Their guide for this part of the festival was a man named Carlos, who had an enthusiastic and joyful energy that made the students instantly feel welcome. Carlos introduced himself and explained that he was passionate about how games and sports brought people together. "No matter where you go," he said, "you'll find people who enjoy playing games, whether they're children or adults. Games are a way to bond, to challenge ourselves, and to celebrate the joy of movement."

The first activity Carlos introduced was a game from Southeast Asia called takraw, which involved a woven ball that players kept in the air using only their feet, knees, chest, and head—no hands allowed.

THE BIG FIELD TRIP

The students watched, fascinated, as Carlos demonstrated a few moves, keeping the small, lightweight ball bouncing effortlessly from one part of his body to another. It looked challenging, but he encouraged the students to try it in pairs, explaining that takraw was all about teamwork, agility, and focus.

Jackson and Ethan volunteered first, both eager to test their skills. They started off a bit clumsily, each trying to keep the ball in the air while learning to pass it back and forth. It was harder than it looked; they quickly realized that it required both balance and cooperation. After a few attempts, they managed to keep the ball bouncing between them a few times without dropping it, and they high-fived each other in excitement. Jackson wrote in his notebook, "Teamwork makes everything better," realizing that takraw was not just about individual skill but about working together to achieve a shared goal.

Next, Carlos introduced the class to a game from West Africa called "Ampe." In Ampe, players stood face to face, clapped their hands, and then jumped into the air, landing with one foot forward. The goal was for each player to guess which foot their partner would land on, making it a game of anticipation and quick reactions. The students took turns playing, laughing as they tried to predict each other's moves and cheered when they guessed correctly.

Sophia loved the game's simplicity, and she felt connected to her classmates as they laughed and clapped along with each round. She realized that sometimes the most enjoyable games were the ones that didn't require any equipment or complicated rules. Ampe was about rhythm, timing, and the joy of shared movement. In her notebook, she wrote, "Games don't need fancy rules—just connection," appreciating how something as simple as jumping and clapping could create such joy and excitement.

Carlos then guided the students to a section of the field where a version of a Scottish game called caber toss was set up, but with lighter, smaller logs that they could handle safely. The caber toss required participants to lift a long log, balance it, and then try to throw it forward so that it flipped end over end. It was challenging, requiring strength, balance, and technique, and the students were eager to give it a try. Carlos explained that in traditional Scottish games, the caber toss was a way for people to show their strength and endurance, a celebration of physical skill.

Emma, who had never tried anything like it before, volunteered to go first. She lifted the log carefully, concentrating as she tried to find her balance. With some encouragement from Carlos and her classmates, she managed to lift and toss it forward, watching in excitement as it flipped halfway over. Her friends cheered, and she felt a surge of pride in herself for trying something new and challenging. She wrote in her notebook, "Games push us to be strong and brave," understanding that games could be a way to test her limits and feel a sense of accomplishment.

The next game Carlos introduced was a traditional Native American game called "stickball." In stickball, players used sticks to carry and throw a small ball toward a goal. The game was similar to modern lacrosse but with simpler rules and equipment. Carlos explained that stickball was often played as a community event, bringing people together and strengthening bonds. The game required agility, focus, and teamwork, and the students quickly paired up to play, each team strategizing on how to reach the goal.

Mia, who was usually shy, surprised herself by getting fully involved in the game. She found that when she focused on passing the ball and working with her teammates, her nerves disappeared. She loved the feeling of being part of a team, each player's strengths contributing to their progress toward the goal. Afterward, she wrote in her notebook, "Team games bring out our best," realizing that sports could help her build confidence and find strength in cooperation.

The students then moved on to a section where Carlos taught them a game called peteca, which originated in Brazil. Peteca was played by hitting a large shuttlecock-like object with the hand, trying to keep it in the air as long as possible or to pass it over a net to an opponent. Carlos explained that peteca combined elements of volleyball and badminton, requiring coordination, timing, and quick reflexes. The students were intrigued by the unusual design of the shuttlecock, and they lined up eagerly to give it a try.

Ethan and Jackson paired up again, enjoying the challenge of keeping the peteca in the air. They quickly found that they had to be alert and quick, adjusting their movements to keep it from hitting the ground. The game was fast-paced and exciting, and they laughed as they passed it back and forth, each one determined not to let it fall. Ethan wrote in his notebook, "Games make us stay sharp," appreciating how peteca challenged his mind and body to work together.

One of the final games Carlos introduced was a relay race inspired by traditional games from various cultures. The students were divided into teams, each team responsible for carrying an object, like a small basket, from one point to another before passing it to the next teammate. Carlos explained that relay races were often played as part of community events, celebrating cooperation, trust, and the shared goal of crossing the finish line together.

Chapter 20: Culinary Traditions and Cooking Together

As the afternoon sunlight began to soften, Ms. Lopez gathered her students once again to guide them toward one of the final experiences of the festival. After exploring games, arts, music, and stories, they were about to embark on a culinary journey that would allow them to taste, smell, and learn about the world through food. This part of the festival was dedicated to culinary traditions, with a section set up to showcase cooking styles and flavors from different cultures. The air was filled with a delicious mix of scents—spices, roasting vegetables, fresh herbs, and baked bread—that made everyone's stomachs rumble in anticipation.

The students noticed that small stations had been arranged in a circle, each one representing a different type of cuisine. There were tables covered in bowls of colorful ingredients, with fresh vegetables, herbs, spices, and grains set out for cooking. At each station, there was a chef ready to teach them about the unique aspects of their cuisine, each excited to share the flavors and techniques that made their food special.

Their guide for this experience was a woman named Leena, who introduced herself with a warm smile and an apron dusted with flour. She explained that food wasn't just something people ate to survive; it was a way to show love, to connect with others, and to carry on traditions. "Cooking together is one of the oldest forms of sharing," she said. "In every culture, food has a way of bringing people together, teaching us about patience, creativity, and generosity." She invited the students to explore the stations and try their hands at preparing different dishes, encouraging them to learn not just about the ingredients, but about the stories behind each one.

The first station they visited featured a type of flatbread that was common in many parts of the world. The chef showed them how to mix flour, water, and a pinch of salt, kneading the dough with care before rolling it out into thin circles. He explained that flatbread was often served with meals, a staple that was both simple and essential in many cultures. The students took turns rolling out the dough, enjoying the feel of it under their hands. They learned how to press it just right to get the perfect thickness, and as they watched the bread cook on a hot griddle, they saw it puff up and brown.

Emma felt a sense of pride as she held up her finished piece of flatbread. She couldn't believe that something so simple could be so satisfying to make. As she tasted the warm, soft bread, she understood why it was considered a staple in so many places. She wrote in her notebook, "Food connects us to the basics," realizing that sometimes the most nourishing foods were also the simplest.

Next, they moved on to a station where a chef was preparing a dish with rice, vegetables, and spices, filling the air with a mouthwatering aroma. The chef explained that rice was a fundamental part of many cuisines, often paired with different ingredients and spices to create countless variations. He showed them how to rinse the rice and sauté vegetables, adding fragrant spices like turmeric, cumin, and coriander. The students were fascinated by how quickly the ingredients came together, each one adding color, flavor, and depth to the dish.

Ethan, who loved trying new foods, was particularly captivated by the spices. He enjoyed the process of sprinkling them into the pan, watching as they transformed the dish into something vibrant and aromatic. When he tasted a spoonful of the finished rice, he was amazed at how each spice contributed to the overall flavor, creating a warm and comforting taste. He wrote in his notebook, "Spices make food come alive," understanding that even a simple dish like rice could be full of excitement when enhanced with the right flavors.

At the next station, they learned how to make dumplings, a dish common in many different cultures but prepared in unique ways depending on where it was made. The chef taught them how to fill small circles of dough with a mixture of vegetables, folding and pinching the edges to create little pockets. She explained that dumplings were often shared among family members, a dish that required everyone's participation, from making the dough to filling and shaping each piece.

Mia loved the process of folding the dumplings, finding it calming and enjoyable. She realized that making dumplings was not just about cooking—it was about working together, each person adding their own touch to the meal. She felt a sense of accomplishment when she saw her neatly folded dumplings lined up on the tray, ready to be steamed. As she tasted one, she thought about the many families around the world who shared this same experience, making and enjoying dumplings together. She wrote in her notebook, "Cooking can be a family tradition," appreciating the way food brought people closer.

Moving along, they reached a station where a chef was making a type of soup that was rich, hearty, and filled with root vegetables and beans. He explained that soups and stews were a part of many cultures, often made with local ingredients and simmered slowly to create deep, comforting flavors. The chef invited the students to chop carrots, onions, and potatoes, showing them how to add each ingredient at the right time to build layers of flavor.

Jackson enjoyed the process of chopping vegetables, finding rhythm and focus in the simple task. He realized that making soup required patience, each ingredient contributing to the final taste. As he tasted the finished soup, he appreciated the warmth and depth of the flavors, understanding why it was considered comfort food in many places. He wrote in his notebook, "Cooking teaches patience and care," seeing that food wasn't just about eating but also about nurturing and taking time to create something meaningful.

At another station, they learned how to make a fresh salad with greens, tomatoes, cucumbers, and a dressing made from lemon juice, olive oil, and herbs. The chef explained that salads were a common way to celebrate fresh ingredients, each vegetable bringing its own taste and texture. She encouraged the students to add their own touch, choosing the ingredients they liked best and experimenting with different combinations.

Sophia loved the colors and freshness of the salad, feeling a sense of joy as she assembled her own bowl. She realized that even something as simple as a salad could be beautiful, each vegetable bringing a burst of color and flavor. When she tasted it, she appreciated the brightness and simplicity, understanding that fresh ingredients didn't need much to shine. She wrote in her notebook, "Food can be vibrant and simple," realizing that the natural flavors of ingredients could be a celebration on their own.

Chapter 21: Festivals of Light and Color

The day was winding down, but the festival still had one last surprise for Ms. Lopez's class. After spending hours exploring food, music, crafts, games, and poetry, they were led toward an area filled with lanterns, candles, and colorful decorations hanging from trees and posts. This area was dedicated to the theme of light and color in celebrations—a section of the festival showcasing different cultural festivals that used lights, colors, and decorations to bring people together in joy, remembrance, and hope.

Ms. Lopez gathered her students around, her face illuminated by the soft glow of lanterns hanging nearby. She explained that around the world, people celebrated festivals that used light and color as symbols of life, love, and renewal. "These festivals," she said, "are about finding hope in the dark, joy in simple things, and unity in community. Light and color have a special way of lifting our spirits, of making the world feel brighter and more connected."

Their guide for this part of the festival was a woman named Amina, who wore a shawl decorated with shimmering patterns that reflected the light around them. Amina welcomed the students and explained that they were about to experience how different cultures used light and color to celebrate special occasions. She explained that in many traditions, light represented hope and renewal, while colors were a way to express happiness, warmth, and unity.

The first section they visited was dedicated to lantern festivals. Amina explained that lanterns were used in celebrations across the world, often symbolizing guidance, wishes, and the beauty of light in darkness. There were paper lanterns of all shapes and sizes, some round and simple, others decorated with intricate patterns. Amina invited the students to create their own lanterns, showing them how to fold paper, decorate it, and add small battery-powered lights inside. As they worked, she explained that lantern festivals were about bringing people together, each light representing a hope or wish for the future.

Mia was fascinated by the process, carefully choosing colors and patterns for her lantern. She decided to write a small wish inside, a message of hope for her family and friends. As she finished and lit her lantern, she felt a sense of warmth and joy, knowing that her small light would join many others to create something beautiful. She wrote in her notebook, "Light is a symbol of hope," feeling inspired by the idea that something as simple as a lantern could carry so much meaning.

Next, Amina led them to a section where large, colorful banners and flags fluttered in the wind. This area was dedicated to the Holi festival, a celebration of colors that marked the arrival of spring in certain cultures. Amina explained that during Holi, people gathered to throw vibrant powders at each other, filling the air with color and joy. The festival was a way to celebrate renewal, friendship, and the beauty of life's colors. The students were given handfuls of colored powders and invited to play, tossing the colors into the air and onto each other.

Ethan immediately jumped into the activity, laughing as he threw a handful of blue powder into the air. His friends joined in, each one splashing colors and sharing in the excitement. By the time they were done, they were covered in a rainbow of colors, their laughter ringing through the air. Ethan wrote in his notebook, "Color makes life joyful," realizing that color could lift spirits and create moments of pure happiness.

As they dusted off, Amina introduced them to another tradition—the lighting of candles for a holiday known as Diwali, the Festival of Lights. She explained that during Diwali, people lit small candles called diyas to symbolize the victory of light over darkness, good over evil, and hope over despair. She invited each student to light a diya and place it in a small pool of water, allowing the soft lights to float and reflect on the water's surface. Amina explained that each candle was like a small beacon, a reminder that light could overcome even the deepest darkness.

Emma felt a deep sense of peace as she placed her diya in the water, watching the small flame flicker gently. She thought about what light meant to her, about the warmth and comfort it brought to dark times. As she watched the candles float, she felt a sense of calm and hope, understanding why people celebrated light in times of darkness. She wrote in her notebook, "Light can bring comfort and courage," feeling that she had glimpsed the meaning behind this simple yet profound ritual.

They moved on to another section where there was a large mandala made from colored sands and flower petals. Amina explained that mandalas were a part of many cultural and spiritual celebrations, symbolizing unity, the universe, and the cycle of life. She invited the students to add their own designs to the mandala, showing them how to create patterns using the sand and petals. Each student took a handful of color and carefully added it to the mandala, creating new shapes and patterns alongside their friends.

Sophia loved the meditative process of creating the mandala, feeling connected to the beauty of each design and color. She realized that the mandala was like a community—each person contributing their own piece to make something beautiful and complete. She wrote in her notebook, "Beauty comes from unity," appreciating the way everyone's work came together to create something whole.

Amina then led the students to a section filled with small fireworks and sparklers, explaining that in many places, fireworks were used to celebrate special occasions, marking the night sky with bursts of light and color. She handed out sparklers to the students and showed them how to safely hold and light them. As they waved their sparklers through the air, they left trails of light, creating shapes and letters that danced in the darkness.

Jackson felt a rush of excitement as he held his sparkler, watching the bright, twinkling light it created. He felt as though he was part of something magical, the darkness around him illuminated by tiny sparks. As the sparkler fizzled out, he thought about how light could create joy and wonder, even for just a moment. He wrote in his notebook, "Light can create magic," realizing that celebrations were a way to bring people together in shared joy.

The students then moved to a quieter area where lanterns floated on a small pond, each one carrying a message written by the person who had released it. Amina explained that in some cultures, people used floating lanterns as a way to remember loved ones, to send messages to those far away, or to release hopes and dreams into the world. She handed each student a lantern and invited them to write a message or a wish before placing it on the water.

Chapter 22: Dance and Movement as Celebration

The class had experienced so much already, and it was hard to believe there could be more. Yet, as they approached the next part of the festival, a wave of energy and excitement filled the air. They heard the sound of music—drums, flutes, and rhythmic beats—echoing from the tents ahead, and saw people of all ages moving together in lively, flowing steps. This was the section of the festival dedicated to dance and movement, and it celebrated the way people around the world expressed joy, tradition, and community through dance.

Ms. Lopez gathered her students at the edge of an open space where performers were moving in vibrant, synchronized steps. Each dancer wore colorful, flowing clothing that seemed to dance along with them, creating an enchanting swirl of color and motion. Ms. Lopez explained that dance was a universal form of expression, used in every culture to celebrate, to mourn, to tell stories, and to come together. "Dance speaks to something deep inside of us," she said, "It allows us to express things we might not be able to put into words."

Their guide for this part of the festival was a man named Rafael, who wore traditional clothing that was both simple and elegant. He welcomed the students with a warm smile and explained that dance was one of the oldest and most joyful ways that people connected with each other. "In every culture," he said, "dance is a way to tell stories, to celebrate, and to remember. Dance brings us together and allows us to feel part of something larger."

Rafael invited the students to watch a performance from a group that danced to rhythms created by drums and clapping hands. The dancers moved gracefully yet powerfully, each step following the beat as though they were part of one single heartbeat. The students watched, mesmerized by the way the dancers seemed to express strength, joy, and unity with each movement. Rafael explained that this dance came from a culture where drums were considered sacred, and dance was a way to honor the rhythm of life itself.

Mia felt a strong sense of connection to the dancers, inspired by the beauty and power of their movements. She realized that dance was more than just moving to music; it was a way to become part of something timeless and meaningful. As she watched, she felt her own feet tapping to the beat, as if her body wanted to join in. She wrote in her notebook, "Dance is a shared heartbeat," understanding that rhythm and movement could create a powerful bond.

Next, Rafael introduced the students to a traditional circle dance that was common in many cultures. He explained that circle dances were often used to bring communities together, as everyone joined hands and moved in a continuous loop. The students were invited to form a circle and join in, each one holding the hand of the person next to them. Rafael showed them simple steps, encouraging them to move with the beat and to feel the energy of the group.

Emma loved the feeling of holding hands with her classmates, each person moving in harmony with the next. As they moved together, she felt a sense of unity and connection, as though they were all part of something greater than themselves. She could feel the strength and warmth of the group, each step creating a sense of togetherness that words couldn't capture. She wrote in her notebook, "Dancing together brings unity," realizing that the circle dance was a way to celebrate community and friendship.

The next dance Rafael introduced was a style of dance that used colorful scarves, each dancer holding one in each hand as they moved. The scarves floated and twirled in the air, adding color and fluidity to the dance. Rafael explained that in some cultures, scarves were used in dances to represent the elements—wind, water, and fire. He showed the students how to hold the scarves, how to let them flow with each movement, creating shapes and patterns in the air.

Ethan was fascinated by the scarves, enjoying the way they seemed to bring his movements to life. He twirled and spun, watching as the colors blurred together, feeling like he was painting in the air. The scarves added a layer of expression to the dance, allowing him to imagine that he was part of the elements themselves. He wrote in his notebook, "Dance can make us feel free," feeling that the scarves allowed him to express something beyond words.

Rafael then demonstrated a dance that involved rhythmic stomping and clapping, each sound adding to the beat of the music. He explained that this type of dance was often used to mark important occasions, like a wedding or a harvest celebration. The students joined in, following Rafael's lead as they stomped, clapped, and moved in time with the music. Each sound they made added to the rhythm, creating a powerful, unified beat that filled the air.

Jackson loved the strength and energy of the dance, feeling the vibrations of each stomp and clap in his chest. He realized that dance wasn't just about movement—it was about sound and rhythm, each beat adding to the feeling of unity. He wrote in his notebook, "Dance lets us feel powerful," understanding that movement and rhythm could be a way to celebrate strength and joy.

The students then moved to another section where Rafael introduced them to a type of partner dance. He explained that partner dances were often about trust and cooperation, each person relying on the other to create smooth, flowing movements. He showed them a few basic steps, encouraging them to find a partner and try moving together. Each pair worked together, laughing and learning as they tried to match each other's steps.

Mia found herself partnered with Jackson, and at first, they struggled to match their movements. But as they practiced, they began to find a rhythm, each one adapting to the other's movements. Mia realized that partner dancing was about more than just moving together—it was about feeling connected, supporting each other's movements, and creating something beautiful together. She wrote in her notebook, "Dance is about trust and connection," appreciating the way dancing with a partner taught her to work in harmony.

Chapter 23: Storytelling Circles and Shared Wisdom

The sky was turning a soft shade of pink as the day at the multicultural festival drew closer to an end. Ms. Lopez's class had danced, cooked, created art, and played games, each experience filling them with new perspectives and joys. But there was one final stop on their journey through the festival—one that promised to bring them even closer together through shared experiences and stories. This area was set up as a storytelling circle, a place where people gathered to listen, learn, and share tales, wisdom, and memories from their lives and cultures. It was designed to feel cozy and inviting, with soft blankets and cushions arranged in a circle under a canopy of twinkling lights.

Ms. Lopez gathered her students and explained that storytelling was one of the most ancient traditions, a way for people to pass down knowledge, values, and memories. She encouraged them to listen carefully, to open their hearts, and to feel the stories as they were told. "Today, you'll hear stories that come from many places, each one carrying a piece of wisdom or a moment worth remembering," she said. "Stories bring us together, helping us understand each other, ourselves, and the world in ways that words alone can't always capture."

Their guide for this part of the festival was an elderly man named Haruto, who sat comfortably on a cushion, his kind eyes twinkling with warmth and wisdom. Haruto welcomed them to the circle with a gentle nod and explained that storytelling was about more than just sharing events—it was about connecting with others, sharing a part of oneself, and inviting listeners to see the world from a new perspective. "Every story," he said, "is like a gift, a piece of the storyteller's heart given to those who listen."

He invited the students to sit and make themselves comfortable as he prepared to share the first story. The students settled in, feeling the anticipation in the air, sensing that they were about to experience something special.

Haruto began with a story from his childhood, a tale his grandmother had told him about a wise fox who lived in a forest and helped travelers find their way home. The fox was known for her kindness, always guiding people through the woods and showing them the safest paths. One night, a terrible storm struck, and a young girl found herself lost in the dark. The wise fox appeared, guiding her through the forest, but she did not ask for anything in return. Instead, she simply said, "One day, help someone in need, just as I have helped you." The girl grew up remembering the fox's words and spent her life helping others, passing on the kindness she had received.

The students listened closely, each one feeling the gentle warmth of the fox's story. Mia, especially, was touched by the idea of kindness without expectation, feeling that it was a beautiful reminder to help others selflessly. She wrote in her notebook, "Kindness needs no reward," understanding that true kindness was a gift given freely, without expecting anything in return.

After Haruto's story, he invited a young woman named Suri to share a story from her culture. Suri spoke softly, her voice weaving a story about a mountain that was sacred to her people. In her story, the mountain was home to spirits who watched over the valley, protecting it and guiding the people. The mountain was said to be a place of wisdom, where people came to seek answers and find peace. The story described how each visitor brought something small to leave on the mountain—a stone, a flower, or even a whispered wish—as a sign of respect and gratitude. The mountain, in return, blessed them with strength and clarity for their journey ahead.

Emma felt deeply connected to the mountain's story, sensing the peace and wisdom it represented. She imagined people climbing the mountain, each one leaving behind a piece of themselves, each one finding a moment of peace. She wrote in her notebook, "Wisdom can be found in quiet places," understanding that sometimes the most profound lessons came from moments of reflection and respect for the world around them.

Next, a man named Tomas shared a story from his homeland about a magical tree that bore golden fruit. According to the story, the tree had the power to grant a wish to those who truly believed in its magic. People would come from far and wide, each one hoping to make a wish. But the tree only granted wishes to those who were humble, kind, and selfless. Many tried and failed, but one day, a young boy came to the tree, not to make a wish for himself but to ask for his sick mother's health. The tree, moved by his selflessness, granted his wish, and the boy's mother recovered.

Ethan was moved by the story of the magical tree, inspired by the boy's selflessness and love for his mother. He thought about how wishes and dreams often focused on helping others, on thinking beyond oneself. He wrote in his notebook, "True wishes are for others," realizing that the most powerful dreams were the ones that included kindness and compassion for those around him.

After Tomas, an older woman named Amara told a story about a river that ran through her village. The river was known as the River of Stories, for it was believed that the river carried the memories and voices of those who had lived before. People would sit by the river's edge, listening to the sound of the water and reflecting on their lives. According to the story, the river would offer guidance to those who listened with an open heart, reminding them of their own strength and resilience.

Jackson found himself captivated by the idea of the River of Stories, imagining the voices and memories carried along by the current. He thought about how listening could help him find wisdom, that paying attention to the world around him could guide him through challenges. He wrote in his notebook, "Wisdom flows like a river," feeling that the story had given him a new perspective on the importance of being present and attentive.

As the evening went on, Haruto shared another story, this time a story of bravery. It was about a young warrior who had to climb a mountain to retrieve a special flower that would cure his village of a terrible illness. The journey was dangerous, and many had warned him not to go. But the young warrior was determined to help his people, facing challenges along the way. When he finally reached the flower, he was exhausted, but he gathered his strength and returned to his village with the cure. The story ended with the warrior passing on the lesson that courage was not the absence of fear but the decision to move forward despite it.

Liam was inspired by the story of the brave warrior, realizing that bravery wasn't about being fearless—it was about facing his fears with determination. He wrote in his notebook, "Bravery is moving forward despite fear," understanding that true courage meant standing strong, even in difficult times.

Suri then shared a story from her culture about a family of birds who migrated together each winter. The family would fly over mountains, rivers, and valleys, relying on each other for guidance and strength. The youngest bird, new to the journey, often grew tired, but the older birds would circle back, encouraging him and showing him the way. The story was a lesson in loyalty and support, a reminder that family and friends could help each other through life's challenges.

Chapter 24: Language, Laughter, and Connection

As the festival drew to its final moments, Ms. Lopez and her class arrived at an area filled with laughter, words, and a joyful energy that seemed to reach everyone in the space. This section of the festival was dedicated to the celebration of languages, laughter, and the simple joys of human connection. It wasn't a quiet area; instead, it was alive with voices, sounds, and expressions that crossed language barriers, reminding everyone that communication was more than words.

Ms. Lopez explained to her students that language, laughter, and gestures were powerful ways to connect with others. "In every part of the world, people find ways to communicate. We share words, but we also share smiles, laughter, and moments of joy that transcend words. Even without speaking the same language, we can find ways to understand each other." The students felt a sense of excitement as they realized that they were about to experience connection in a way that went beyond words.

Their guide for this section was a young woman named Leila, whose enthusiasm was contagious. She had traveled around the world, learning different languages and discovering the ways people communicated across cultures. She explained that while words were important, there were many ways to connect with others, whether through a shared smile, a kind gesture, or a simple laugh. "Laughter, for example, is universal," she said. "People laugh everywhere, and laughter is a bridge that connects us, even when words fail."

The first activity Leila introduced was a game designed to break down language barriers. She invited the students to pair up with someone they didn't usually talk to and gave each pair a set of cards with images, colors, and symbols. The students were asked to communicate a story or a memory using only the cards, without speaking. The idea was to use gestures, facial expressions, and the symbols on the cards to convey their story.

Mia paired up with Jackson, feeling a little nervous but excited. She chose a few cards that reminded her of a family camping trip, showing mountains, stars, and a small tent. She used her hands to mimic a campfire, her eyes wide with excitement as she tried to convey the feeling of being outdoors. Jackson watched closely, nodding as he pieced together the story. He smiled, understanding her memory without needing any words. Mia wrote in her notebook, "Communication is more than words," realizing that she could share moments and emotions even without speaking.

Next, Leila introduced the students to a language-matching game. She handed out small cards, each one with a word written in a different language, such as "hello," "love," "friend," and "peace." The students were encouraged to find their matching card by asking each other for help. They quickly discovered that some words looked familiar, while others were entirely new. They found themselves laughing as they tried to pronounce each word, learning from each other and sharing the joy of discovery.

Ethan laughed as he attempted to pronounce a greeting in a language he had never heard before. He was surprised to find that, despite his struggle, the person he asked recognized the word and matched it to its meaning. He felt a spark of joy, realizing that learning a new word was like finding a key to another person's world. He wrote in his notebook, "Language opens doors to understanding," appreciating the excitement of learning words from different languages and how they connected him to others.

After the matching game, Leila introduced the students to the art of storytelling with sounds and gestures. She explained that in some cultures, people used sounds, body movements, and facial expressions to tell stories, especially when words weren't enough or when they wanted to express something more playful. She encouraged each student to create a short story, using only sounds and movements to bring it to life.

Sophia, who was usually shy, felt inspired to try this storytelling technique. She thought of a story about a rainy day, using her hands to imitate raindrops falling and tapping her fingers on the floor to create the sound of rain. She made a swooshing sound to represent the wind and a loud clap to mimic thunder. Her classmates watched, smiling as they pieced together her story, enjoying the creativity and energy in her performance. Sophia wrote in her notebook, "Stories can be told without words," feeling proud that she could share her ideas in a new and expressive way.

Leila then brought the students together for a game she called "Laughter Yoga." She explained that laughter yoga was a practice from a part of the world where people believed that laughter had the power to heal, to reduce stress, and to bring people together. She asked the students to start by taking a deep breath, then to laugh as loudly and joyfully as they could, even if it felt a bit silly. At first, the laughter felt forced, but soon, the students found themselves genuinely laughing, their giggles contagious as they fed off each other's joy.

Jackson found himself laughing until his cheeks hurt, feeling a lightness he hadn't expected. He realized that laughter didn't need a reason—it was simply a way to let go of worries, to connect, and to enjoy the present moment. He wrote in his notebook, "Laughter connects us beyond words," appreciating the way laughter filled the air and brought everyone closer.

The students then participated in an activity where they learned how to say "hello" in several different languages. Leila explained that greetings were a powerful way to bridge cultures, a simple gesture that conveyed respect, warmth, and curiosity. She demonstrated how to say "hello" in various languages, encouraging the students to try each one. Some were similar to what they already knew, while others were entirely new.

Emma was intrigued by the idea of greetings, realizing that something as simple as a "hello" could open doors and create friendships. She enjoyed the challenge of learning each greeting, her heart warming as she imagined the people who used these words every day. She wrote in her notebook, "A greeting is a gift of connection," feeling that she had learned a small but meaningful way to connect with people around the world.

In the next activity, Leila taught the students a few traditional hand gestures and symbols used in different cultures to express gratitude, respect, or greeting. She explained that gestures often carried deep meaning, that in some places, a bow or a simple hand movement could convey respect, welcome, or joy. She demonstrated each gesture carefully, and the students mirrored her movements, each one feeling the significance of these simple acts.

Mia loved learning the different gestures, feeling that each one connected her to something beyond words. She practiced a bow that symbolized respect, her movements slow and intentional. She realized that these gestures were a language of their own, each one carrying the weight of culture and tradition. She wrote in her notebook, "Gestures are a language of respect," appreciating the grace and meaning in each movement.

Leila then introduced them to the idea of "body language" and how it played a role in communication everywhere, often unconsciously. She encouraged the students to try communicating through only their body language—postures, facial expressions, and eye contact. They worked in pairs, each one attempting to convey emotions like happiness, surprise, curiosity, or sadness without speaking. It was challenging, but soon they began to notice the nuances in each other's expressions and movements.

Liam was surprised by how much he could understand through body language. He realized that sometimes, words weren't necessary to understand someone's feelings. He wrote in his notebook, "Body language speaks when words can't," understanding that people could connect deeply even without saying anything.

For the last activity, Leila led the students in a song that used sounds and rhythms from different languages. She explained that music was one of the most universal forms of connection, a way for people to share emotions and stories even without understanding each other's words. The students followed along, clapping their hands, humming, and singing the sounds, each one contributing to the rhythm. They could feel the harmony, each sound blending with the others, creating a shared energy that connected them all.

Chapter 25: The Closing Circle of Gratitude

As the sun began to set on their unforgettable day, Ms. Lopez gathered her students one last time. Their faces were flushed with excitement, and their notebooks were filled with thoughts, memories, and lessons from the festival. They had shared laughter, stories, music, dance, food, and culture from around the world. Ms. Lopez saw the joy and wonder in their expressions and knew that they had each gained something invaluable, a gift that would stay with them long after they left the festival grounds. But before they departed, she wanted to bring everyone together in a final moment of reflection and gratitude.

They walked together to a quiet clearing where a circle of cushions awaited them. Ms. Lopez encouraged each student to find a place in the circle and explained that this last gathering was called a Circle of Gratitude. In many cultures, people closed important experiences with a moment of gratitude, sharing thoughts and reflections to honor the day. Ms. Lopez explained that gratitude could be a powerful way to express appreciation, to remember the lessons learned, and to acknowledge the people and moments that had touched their hearts.

The students looked around the circle, feeling a mixture of anticipation and contentment. Ms. Lopez asked each of them to share something they were grateful for or a lesson they had learned that they wanted to carry with them. She invited them to speak from the heart, encouraging them to express whatever felt meaningful or true to them in that moment.

Mia was the first to speak, and though she felt a bit nervous, she took a deep breath and looked around the circle, finding comfort in the familiar faces of her classmates. She shared how grateful she was for the opportunity to experience so many different cultures in one day, to learn things that made her see the world in a new light. She talked about how the day had taught her that everyone had something special to share, a unique story or talent that enriched the lives of others. She wrote in her notebook, "Everyone's story adds beauty to the world," realizing that each culture, each person, had something valuable to offer.

Ethan spoke next, his voice filled with excitement as he recounted the many flavors, games, and traditions he had experienced. He talked about how much he had enjoyed trying new foods and learning the stories behind each dish. He expressed gratitude for the people who had welcomed him into their world through food, showing him that something as simple as a meal could carry deep meaning and connection. "Food is a bridge to understanding," he said, feeling a newfound appreciation for the ways that people shared their heritage and love through cooking.

Emma followed, her face glowing as she reflected on the moments of music and dance. She described how each rhythm and movement had opened her heart, showing her the joy and unity that came from dancing together. She talked about the power of music to connect people, to make them feel part of something larger than themselves. She was grateful for the experience, for the way it had shown her that music was more than just sound—it was a way to express emotions, to celebrate, and to bring people together. "Music connects us to each other," she said, feeling a deep appreciation for the power of rhythm and melody to create unity.

Jackson was next, and he spoke about the strength he had felt from the games and physical activities they had tried. He shared how each game had taught him something about cooperation, resilience, and determination. He was grateful for the lessons he had learned about teamwork and trust, about relying on others and working together toward a common goal. "We're stronger together," he said, realizing that the true strength of any community came from the connections people built with one another.

Sophia, who had been a bit quieter throughout the day, surprised herself by speaking up. She shared how much she had enjoyed the arts and crafts, the colors, and the symbols she had seen throughout the festival. She was grateful for the beauty she had experienced, for the way it had opened her eyes to the different ways people expressed themselves and told their stories. She felt a sense of awe at the thought of how art could be a language, a way for people to communicate their thoughts, dreams, and memories. "Art is a language we all share," she said, feeling that the day had inspired her to look at creativity as a universal gift.

Liam talked about the stories he had heard and the storytellers he had met. He spoke about how each story had carried a lesson, a piece of wisdom that could guide him through life. He was grateful for the way storytelling had shown him that wisdom wasn't something found only in books—it was something shared, passed down, and cherished. "Stories are gifts of wisdom," he said, realizing that he would carry the lessons of the stories with him, each one a small light to guide him.

Mia then shared her thoughts on the final circle of laughter and communication they had shared, how she had learned that connection went beyond language, that smiles and gestures could carry meaning and warmth. She was grateful for the joy she had felt in the simple act of laughing and connecting, realizing that kindness and openness were languages anyone could understand. "Connection doesn't need words," she said, feeling that this experience had shown her the beauty of reaching out and understanding one another in new ways.

Ethan spoke again, adding how grateful he was for the experience of seeing everyone come together, each person with their own stories, backgrounds, and traditions, yet all sharing a sense of unity and joy. He talked about how it had made him feel part of something bigger, connected to people not only from his own class but from cultures all around the world. "Unity is found in our differences," he said, appreciating that diversity was something to be celebrated, not feared.

Ms. Lopez smiled as she listened to each of her students speak, feeling a deep sense of pride and gratitude for the growth and connection she had witnessed. She shared her own gratitude, telling the students how proud she was of their open hearts and curious minds, how much joy it had brought her to see them embrace each new experience. She encouraged them to remember the lessons of the day, to carry the spirit of the festival with them as they moved forward, to continue learning from others and sharing their own stories.

Before they left, Ms. Lopez invited the students to hold hands and close their eyes for a moment of quiet reflection. She encouraged them to think of one word that represented what they had felt, learned, or appreciated during the festival. She explained that this word would be something they could carry with them as a reminder of the experience, a small piece of wisdom or joy that would stay in their hearts.

As they stood in the circle, each student thought deeply about the day, about the lessons, laughter, and connections they had shared. They felt a sense of calm and unity, a feeling that they were part of something lasting and meaningful. They held their words close, knowing that these words represented their own experiences and the memories they would cherish.

When they opened their eyes, the sky had darkened, and the stars were beginning to twinkle above them. Ms. Lopez looked around the circle, feeling a profound sense of gratitude for each of her students, for the journey they had taken together. She reminded them that while the festival was ending, the lessons they had learned would stay with them, lighting their paths and guiding them in the years to come.

Don't miss out!

Visit the website below and you can sign up to receive emails whenever Arden Willowfield publishes a new book. There's no charge and no obligation.

https://books2read.com/r/B-A-OEIVC-IDNIF

BOOKS 2 READ

Connecting independent readers to independent writers.

Did you love *The Big Field Trip*? Then you should read *Kai's Quest for Harmony*[1] by Sylvia Mooncrest!

Kai's Quest for Harmony is a journey into the heart of nature and beyond, where young Kai embarks on a musical adventure to gather the sounds of the world. From mountains and forests to oceans and stars, Kai discovers the voices of nature and the beauty of diversity. Along the way, he learns valuable lessons about unity, connection, and kindness. Filled with heartwarming encounters, Kai's journey reminds readers that the world is full of unique voices, each contributing to the melody of life. Perfect for inspiring children ages 5-10 to appreciate harmony in all its forms.

---

1. https://books2read.com/u/49qJAW

2. https://books2read.com/u/49qJAW

About the Publisher

Whimsy Tales Press is a creative powerhouse devoted to publishing exceptional children's books that spark joy, imagination, and lifelong learning. With a mission to inspire young minds, the company crafts stories that celebrate diversity, kindness, and the magic of discovery. Whimsy Tales Press collaborates with passionate authors and illustrators to bring captivating characters and enchanting worlds to life. From heartwarming bedtime tales to empowering adventures, every book is designed to entertain while fostering empathy and curiosity. Committed to excellence and inclusivity, Whimsy Tales Press ensures that each story leaves a lasting impression, encouraging children to dream big and believe in endless possibilities.